Cal Ripken, Jr.'s
★ALL★
STARS

Hothead

Hothead

a novel by
CAL RIPKEN, JR.
with Kevin Cowherd

𝒟𝒾𝓈𝓃𝑒𝓎 • Hyperion Books

New York

Thanks to all my wonderful friends at *The Baltimore Sun* for all
their support. And a very special thanks to Stephanie Owens Lurie,
Editorial Director of Disney • Hyperion Books, for her unfailing patience
and optimism, her steady guidance throughout the project, and her
remarkable editing skills. We couldn't have written this book without her.
K. C.

First Disney • Hyperion paperback edition, 2012
10 9 8 7 6 5 4 3 2 1
V475-2873-0-11335
Printed in the United States of America

Library of Congress Control Number: 2011282543
ISBN: 978-1-4231-4003-0

Visit www.disneyhyperionbooks.com

The ball was scorched—Connor Sullivan saw that right away.

It shot past the pitcher on one hop, then headed for the outfield as Connor broke to his left from his shortstop position.

With three strides he was there, lunging at the last minute to glove the ball behind second base. He spun, going with his momentum, and fired a bullet to first.

It beat the Braves runner by a step.

"He's out!" the umpire shouted, pumping his fist.

The packed stands behind home plate exploded with cheers and shouts of "Way to go, Connor!" and "Now let's get some hits, Orioles!"

The Orioles hustled off the field and smacked gloves with Connor near the dugout, the way the big leaguers did after a great play.

"Where base hits go to die!" second baseman Willie Pitts said, grabbing Connor's glove and holding it over his head like a trophy.

"Someone call ESPN!" first baseman Jordy Marsh said.

"Highlights at eleven! Too bad you can't stay up that late, C!"

The rest of the Orioles laughed. This one was all but over. They led the Braves 10–3 in the fifth inning, and the great Connor Sullivan was putting on another show.

He was already 3-for-3 at the plate, including a soaring three-run homer that was probably still being tracked by radar at BWI-Marshall Airport. And he'd made an earlier sparkling play in the field, too, backhanding a line drive in the hole to rob the Braves of another hit.

There was no doubt about it: the Orioles were thankful to have Connor on their team. He was their best player, their all-star shortstop, and a beast of a cleanup hitter.

Tall and broad-shouldered, with a thick mop of brown hair that spilled out from under his cap, he was also their meal ticket if the Orioles planned to win the Dulaney Babe Ruth League championship. And they definitely did, seeing as how they had a perfect 10–0 record with five games to go.

All this could give a kid a big head. But Connor was not that sort of kid.

Sure, he made jokes about having his own posse as a twelve-year-old baseball phenom.

"Jordy, you can be my limo driver," he'd say. "The rest of you, make yourselves useful. Open some doors and keep the paparazzi away."

And he did show up for a game wearing dark, movie-star shades and silver stud earrings—the magnetic kind you get at the dollar store. It cracked up everyone, including his coach, Ray Hammond.

But the rest of the Orioles knew Connor was really the most humble player on the team. He was even more humble than reserve player Marty Loopus, who had a lot to be humble about, seeing as how he couldn't hit, couldn't catch, and couldn't throw.

"He doesn't run too well, either," Willie Pitts pointed out helpfully whenever Marty grounded out weakly to the pitcher, his usual at bat.

The Orioles also knew no one loved baseball more than Connor Sullivan. No one worked harder at the game, either.

The bounce-back net in the Sullivans' backyard was worn and frayed from use. Connor practiced catching fly balls and grounders for hours, all the while ferociously chewing gum and blowing bubbles like one of his idols, Adam Jones, of the big-league Orioles.

On weekends, Connor could always be found at Sports, the big amusement arcade near his home, taking endless cuts in the batting cages.

Lately, in fact, he'd begun to wonder if he wasn't practicing too much.

"Don't try to be perfect, Connor," his dad always said. "Baseball isn't about perfection. Just enjoy the game."

But sometimes that was hard, especially with what was going on at home. These days he'd been feeling more and more frustrated during games.

If I just work harder, Connor found himself thinking, at least I can make Mom and Dad proud, take their minds off their worries.

All this was running through his head in the sixth inning, when the Braves had runners on first and second with two outs. The next batter lifted a lazy fly ball that drifted behind third base.

Connor circled to his right. He had the better angle on the ball and called off third baseman Carlos Molina. "I got it!" Connor yelled, tapping his glove with his fist, wondering if he should do the Adam Jones bubble-blow as the ball floated out of the bright blue May sky.

Then he watched in disbelief as the ball kicked off the heel of his glove and rolled harmlessly to the grass. Carlos hustled to retrieve it, but not before two runs scored.

Instantly, Connor felt something welling up inside him. *How did I blow an easy fly ball like that? I can't even blame the stupid sun!*

Before he could stop himself, he slammed his glove to the ground in disgust. Then, convinced the glove hadn't absorbed enough punishment, he kicked it as hard as he could.

Connor didn't think a battered Wilson glove could travel that far. But this one sailed past the pitcher's mound, where Jordy, his best friend, picked it up with a shocked grin.

"That little act might make *SportsCenter*, bro," Jordy said, handing over the glove. "Good thing the ump had his back turned."

By now, Connor's anger had vanished, replaced by a major case of embarrassment. "With my luck, it'll be all over YouTube, too," he muttered.

Then they heard it.

"CONNOR!"

Coach Hammond's voice cut the air like a whip. He stood

on the dugout steps and glared at his shortstop. "Bring it in, son," he said. Turning to Marty Loopus on the bench, he said, "Marty, you're in for Connor."

Feeling his face redden, Connor trudged to the dugout as a hush fell over the crowd. It was a silence he had never heard before at a baseball game, the kind of silence you felt in a doctor's office right before he gave you a shot.

"Connor, you're better than that," Coach Hammond said gruffly. "And I'm not talking about the error. We don't lose our temper like that. Not on this team."

The rest of the game seemed to take forever. The Orioles held on for a 10–6 win, even with Marty booting a ground ball with a runner on second and air-mailing the throw in the direction of the hot dog stand, allowing another Braves run.

Connor was still thinking about the botched fly ball—he'd never had a meltdown like that in his life—when the two teams lined up to slap hands. And he was still thinking about it when Jordy draped an arm over his shoulder.

"Hey, hothead, we're going for ice cream," Jordy said. "The great Connor Sullivan needs to cool off."

Connor shook his head wearily. He sat down and took off his spikes. "No, I better not," he said. "Same old story: no money."

Jordy smiled and pulled a rumpled five-dollar bill from the top of his sock. "Ta-daaa!" he said. "This'll take care of both of us."

"No, I've been mooching off you guys for weeks," Connor said. "Besides, I have a ton of homework."

Jordy pretended to be astonished. "The great Connor

Sullivan does homework?" he said. "Can't get your posse to do it for you?"

"Gave 'em the night off," Connor said. He managed a weak smile. "Besides, they stink at math."

Jordy shrugged and ran off to join the other Orioles. Connor tossed his spikes, bat, and glove in his equipment bag and slung it over his shoulder. He didn't have a ride, because neither of his parents had come to the game today—which was probably just as well, considering. It would be a long walk home. And he was in no great hurry to get there.

He pictured his mom and dad sitting at the kitchen table, the mail stacked high in front of them. They would open envelopes one by one, punch numbers into the calculator, then sigh and moan, their worried voices muffled for the sake of the kids.

No, bill-paying day was never a fun time in the Sullivan household.

Connor shook his head mournfully and reached for a cheeseburger. His mom was always talking about comfort foods: macaroni and cheese, meat loaf, mashed potatoes. But if there was a better comfort food on this earth than a cheeseburger, Connor had yet to find it—and he was always looking.

"An easy fly ball!" he said between bites. "Can of corn, you'd call it. And I blew it."

"Everyone makes errors, Connor," Bill Sullivan said.

"But everyone doesn't spike his glove in the dirt after that. And kick it halfway to Camden Yards."

"Okay, you got me there."

"I acted like a jerk today," Connor said.

"Agreed. You definitely redlined the jerk-o-meter."

Connor and his dad sat at the patio table in their backyard. The sun was setting, with streaks of yellow and pink running across the sky, as his dad pulled the last of the burgers and fried onions off the hot grill.

Connor's mom was leaving for work, dressed in her blue nurse's scrubs and white sneakers. "The ER will be a zoo tonight," Karen Sullivan said when she stepped outside, car keys in hand. "Saturday night and a full moon? Oh, they'll be wheeling them in like it's an assembly line."

"Need some extra protein for the road?" Connor said, lifting up the platter of cheeseburgers. Karen was on an all-veggie diet, for which her family teased her no end.

"I see you two aren't hung up on cholesterol," she said.

"Or bad breath," his dad said, happily popping a huge slice of burned onion in his mouth.

"Well, I'll catch you two cavemen tomorrow," Karen said with a smile. "Oh, and Connor, I'm sorry again about missing the game today. Life has been so hectic lately." She blew a stray lock of hair out of her face. "I'm glad you're still on a winning streak."

"Don't worry about it, Mom," Connor said, and he meant it. The last thing she needed right now was to see her son wigging out on a baseball field.

"I'm getting the play-by-play now, honey," said Connor's father. "I'll fill you in later."

Connor's big sister, Brianna, was missing this meat-fest too. She was with her friends at the mall, doing whatever fifteen-year-old girls did there, which seemed to be flirting with pimply-faced boys and shopping for cheap earrings, as far as Connor could see.

The truth was, he loved evenings alone with his dad. They talked about everything: TV shows and movies, music, girls, how Connor was doing in seventh grade at York Middle School.

But mostly, at times like this, they talked baseball.

Connor's dad had played shortstop for two years at

the University of Maryland before a shoulder injury cut short his college career. He knew the game inside and out. But Connor loved that he wasn't one of these type A dads who was always going on and on about how great he was back in the day, and who insisted you do everything on the baseball field just the way he did. Only when Connor asked would his dad offer tips on laying down a drag bunt, or the best way to take a lead at first or cross the bag at second on a double play.

Lately, though, his dad was available to talk baseball just about any time—which was the whole problem, when you came right down to it.

Now Connor put down his cheeseburger and wiped his mouth with his napkin. He studied his dad for a moment, trying to gauge his mood. Then he took a deep breath and thought: *And the kid swings for the fences . . .*

"Any luck with the job search?" he said.

His dad gave him a tired smile and shook his head slowly.

"Nothing yet, buddy," he said. "But don't worry. I'll find something soon."

Soon—how many times had Connor heard that? How long had it been now—five months?—since his dad had been laid off from his job as a car salesman at Johnson Chrysler, the big dealership on Route 40? Connor knew his father spent hours each day looking for a new job, but so far things weren't working out. And his mom was taking more shifts in the emergency room just to keep her job, which is why neither had been able to get to a game in weeks.

Money was tight—anyone with eyes could see that. The

family hadn't gone out to eat in months. New clothes, new shoes, his braces—all would have to wait, his parents kept telling him.

Even Brianna seemed stressed lately. To save money, she had started making her own clothes and selling some on Etsy, a Web site for buying and selling handmade items.

Connor took another bite of his burger and glanced at the calendar hanging just inside the screen door. Five weeks until the Brooks Robinson Camp, the most prestigious baseball camp around—by invitation only. Connor had one of those prized invitations with the embossed *BR* seal sitting on his dresser. But where were they going to find money for baseball camp?

"I won't be out of a job forever, bud," his dad said, as if reading his mind. "People aren't buying cars the way they used to. But they say the economy is bouncing back. And we're lucky that your mom makes a decent living. There are lots of folks worse off than we are."

Connor knew his dad was right. But knowing that wasn't helping his mood these days. In fact, it made him feel guilty. He was so embarrassed about his dad being out of work that he hadn't told anyone about it, not even Jordy. Keeping such a big secret—especially from his best friend—didn't feel right. But he couldn't bring himself to do anything else.

Dessert was vanilla ice cream with chocolate syrup. It softened quickly in the humid air outside. Connor thought about all of his friends going out for ice cream without him, and he lost his appetite. He put down his spoon and stared at the milky brown soup in his bowl.

"Still reliving your blowup today?" Connor's dad asked.

Connor just nodded, afraid his voice would crack.

"You talk about a meltdown," his dad said. "I almost went thermonuclear the other day at that job interview."

"The Toyota dealership?" Connor said, glad for the change of subject.

"That's the one. A young guy interviewed me. He was, I don't know, thirty, thirty-one. One of their HR guys. So-o-o condescending. Kept asking about my computer skills. 'Hey, I'm fifty-one,' I told him, 'not a hundred and one. I know this stuff.'"

"Yeah, you're on the computer all the time," Connor agreed. "'Course you're only playing solitaire, but . . .'"

His dad ignored the bait. "No matter what I said—'Sure, I'm up on Microsoft Word, Excel, all that stuff' he'd look at me and smirk, like: 'Whatever you say, geezer.' I was getting angrier and angrier."

"So you reached over and popped him, right?" Connor said with a grin. "Threw an uppercut like your hero Muhammad Ali?"

"Oh, I wanted to, believe me," his dad said. "But I just took a deep breath. And I thought: what good would it do to lose my temper? Would it get me the job? Maybe I'd feel better for five seconds. But then I'd be so ashamed of flipping out, it wouldn't be worth it."

Connor nodded again. Oh, yeah, he thought. You feel pretty ridiculous when it's over.

The sky was getting dark now, the last rays of the sun vanishing behind the tall trees that ringed the Sullivans' backyard.

But it was still warm out, and Connor's dad showed no inclination to head back inside. He ducked into the kitchen and came back out with a cup of coffee.

"Know what I used to do when I was your age and I got angry and frustrated playing ball?" he said, chuckling at the memory. "Push-ups."

Connor was puzzled. "Push-ups?"

"Yep," his dad said. "Nothing wrong with being angry when you make an error or strike out. It shows you care, shows you're passionate about the game. But make that anger work for you. Channel it somehow. Push-ups help you work off that frustration—build up your body, too."

Connor stared at his dad for several seconds. Bill Sullivan was a big man, six feet three and 275 pounds, with a big belly that heaved over his belt. Connor tried to picture his dad as a skinny seventh grader, dropping to the floor of his bedroom and knocking off fifty push-ups after a bad game. It was hard to imagine, all right. The thought made him smile.

His dad gulped some coffee, stood, and began cleaning the grill. "Did I ever tell you about Billy Shindle?" he asked.

"I don't think so," Connor said.

"Billy Shindle was a shortstop for the old Philadelphia Quakers many years ago. We're talking 1890s. He made one hundred twenty-two errors in one season. It's still the major league record."

Connor's eyes widened.

"Yep, one hundred twenty-two errors," his dad said. "Google it if you don't believe me."

"He must have been the worst fielder of all time,"

Connor said. "Even worse than Marty Loopus."

They both laughed.

"The point is," his dad said, "Billy Shindle was a guy who *should* have slammed his glove to the ground. Or thrown it in a garbage can and given up baseball altogether. But not you, Connor. You've always played the game the right way, always made your mom and me proud. There's no reason to lose your cool. Don't worry about errors—you'll be making them as long as you play the game."

With that, he leaned over, kissed Connor on the forehead, and went inside.

In the darkness, Connor thought, Well, I plan to be playing this game a long time. Sometimes, when he closed his eyes at night, he could even see himself on the field in Camden Yards one day.

You wouldn't want to lose your cool there. A baseball cathedral, his dad called it. Having a meltdown there would be a real sin.

The Orioles and Red Sox were just finishing their pregame warm-ups at Eddie Murray Field a few days later when a voice behind the backstop bellowed, "Where's the great Connor Sullivan? I need to talk to him right now."

"Uh-oh, Melissa Morrow," Willie Pitts said to Connor. "I'd recognize that foghorn anywhere."

All Connor knew about Melissa was that the other guys thought she was a big, fat pain in the butt.

Actually, she wasn't big or fat at all, and she could even be considered kind of pretty—if you liked girls with freckles, Chiclets-white teeth, and mounds of red hair. Connor was beginning to think he did.

But Melissa had a way of speaking to you that made you feel dumb—dumber even than Mr. Corbacio made you feel in science class when you messed up on a cells, tissues, and organs quiz. So when she marched up to him waving a notebook, Connor was fully prepared to feel as if his IQ had dropped forty points.

He didn't have to wait long.

"You probably don't know I'm the sports editor of the school newspaper," she began.

"What, you don't think I know how to read?" Connor said.

Melissa didn't miss a beat. "I'm sure you manage to get by—somehow."

"Something I can do for you?" Connor said. "Maybe you noticed we're about to play ball."

Melissa made a big show of looking amazed.

"You mean all these dorky-looking boys in their polyester uniforms, with the bats and the balls and the gloves—they're here to play baseball?"

"Bossy *and* sarcastic—an intoxicating combination," Connor said with a smile. He felt good today, ready to play, encouraged by the pep talk his dad had given him. Even Melissa's presence wasn't going to dampen his mood.

"Look," Melissa said, "I just want you to know we're publishing one more edition of the *York Tattler* before summer vacation."

"Thanks for the memo," Connor said, pulling a bat from his equipment bag. "I'll be sure to pick up a copy. Maybe I'll find someone to read it to me."

"You should," Melissa said. "Because I'm doing a big story on you."

Now it was Connor's turn to look surprised.

"Me?" he said. "Why waste space on me?"

"Oh, come on, Mr. Modest," Melissa said. "Everyone knows you're the best player in the league. Best hitter, best shortstop, surefire all-star, blah, blah, blah. And I hear you're going to the Brooks Robinson camp, too." She smiled and put both hands on her hips, gazing at him intently. "No doubt about it," she went on, "inquiring minds want to know all about the great Connor Sullivan."

For a moment, Connor was speechless. He pretended to examine his bat, waiting for his brain to process what he'd just heard.

"What if I don't want you writing about me?" he said finally.

Melissa shook her head sadly, as if talking to a particularly slow third grader. "Ever hear of the First Amendment, bonehead?" she said. "Freedom of the press? That ring a bell anywhere?"

"Freedom of the press, freedom of the press . . ." Connor said, scratching his head. "No, that's a new one for me."

Melissa shot him a sour look. "Anyway, I'll be coming to the rest of your games," she said. "And I'll be taking pictures for the story and shooting video for our Web site. Probably have to interview you once or twice, too."

Great, Connor thought. A couple more conversations like this and my IQ will be down to zero.

"Nobody wants to read about me, Melissa," he said. "I'm a pretty boring guy."

"Uh-huh. Right," Melissa said.

"Don't believe me?" With that, Connor shouted to Jordy Marsh and Willie Pitts, who were loosening their arms along the sideline. "Guys, aren't I the most boring person you ever met?"

Willie grinned and nodded. "Dude, you're like walking anesthesia," he said.

"You're putting me to sleep right now," Jordy added.

"Nice try, hotshot," Melissa said, poking a finger in Connor's chest. "But you're my *Tattler* story. Go out there and make us both look good."

She turned on her heel, strode over to the bleachers behind home plate, and found a seat. Connor watched her pull a tiny video camera from her backpack and fiddle with the lens.

As the Red Sox took the field, he couldn't decide who was making him more nervous: Melissa Morrow, or the big kid warming up on the mound, Billy Burrell.

If Melissa threw a fastball as hard as Billy did, Connor decided, it would be no contest.

Billy Burrell looked even bigger and older and scarier—if that was possible—than he had the last time he had faced the Orioles.

Warming up on the mound, the Red Sox pitcher appeared to be seven feet tall. His cap was pulled low on his forehead, shading two dark slits that might have been his eyes. His windup was all arms and legs unfolding at crazy angles. And his pitches popped into the catcher's mitt with a loud *THWACK!*

"The boy can bring it a little," Willie Pitts said, leaning on his bat and studying Billy from the on-deck circle.

"Someone check his ID," said Jordy Marsh. "I swear I saw him in a Gillette commercial."

Once the game started, Billy wasted no time showing off his stuff. He got Willie, the O's' leadoff batter, on a bouncer to second base. Carlos Molina struck out on three fastballs. Jordy ran the count to 3 and 2, and struck out on a curveball that seemed to break from somewhere near third base.

As he walked off the mound, Billy stared into the Orioles

dugout. Then he pretended to blow on the smoking barrel of a six-shooter.

"Oooh, we're scared!" yelled Marty Loopus, who actually would have been terrified if he were facing Billy instead of riding the bench.

"Guys, don't pay attention to that garbage," Coach Hammond said. "Just play the game."

Connor looked over at his coach. The guy was as old-school as they came—buzz cut, neatly-trimmed mustache, wearing his signature blue Police Athletic League Wind-breaker, a testament to his twenty-two years on the Baltimore police force. The Orioles knew it drove Coach nuts to see young ballplayers celebrating wildly after a home run or a great catch or a well-pitched inning. The truth was, Coach didn't like them doing anything that could make a player on the other team feel bad. "Showing up the other guy," is what he called it.

Seeing Coach's reaction to Billy's taunts, Connor thought back to an early-season game against the Dodgers. Robbie Hammond, Coach's son and the Orioles' best pitcher, had struck out a batter with the bases loaded to end the inning. As he walked off the mound, Robbie had yelled "Yeah!" and pumped his fist. When Robbie reached the dugout, Coach had gathered the Orioles around him. "If you struck out," he told them, "would you want some knucklehead yelling and pumping his fist at you? Let's play with class, gentlemen."

Robbie had been mortified at his dad's words. He'd hung his head and stared at the cement floor. But Coach had made his point. The Orioles knew better than to do any trash-talking or showboating when he was around.

Billy Burrell, Connor decided, would last about five seconds around Coach.

In the second inning, Connor lined a clean single over Billy's head to start things off. Standing on first, he noticed Billy wasn't doing his smoking–six-gun routine now.

But Robbie followed with a grounder to short that the Red Sox turned into an easy double play. And Yancy Arroyo hit a pop fly to the first baseman to end the inning.

Fortunately for the Orioles, Robbie was pitching pretty well, too, matching Billy in scoreless innings.

It was still 0–0 in the fourth when Willie Pitts drew a walk on four pitches. Billy shook his head in disgust and stared hard at the umpire as Willie trotted down to first.

"This is it, guys!" Marty Loopus yelled. "Mr. Six-Gun is losing it!"

Willie promptly stole second, which seemed to rattle Billy even more. With Carlos Molina at the plate, Billy reared back and threw even harder. The result was another four-pitch walk. Jordy Marsh drew yet a third walk.

Now Billy Burrell was seething.

The Red Sox catcher, a pudgy kid named Dylan, walked out to the mound to try to settle him down.

"Get back behind the plate, fat boy," Billy snarled, and Dylan quickly retreated.

Bases loaded. No outs. In the dugout, the Orioles came to life. They hooted and cheered and banged their bats against the bench as Connor strolled to the plate.

"Here we go, C!" Yancy Arroyo yelled.

"Wait for your pitch, Connor!" Coach Hammond shouted.

Connor stepped into the batter's box. Slowly he dug one

spike into the dirt and then the other. Then he tapped the far corner of the plate with his bat, assuring himself he could reach an outside pitch. What was it his dad always said? Act like you own the batter's box. This is your office. Go to work.

Billy glared at him. He got the sign from his catcher, went into his windup, and threw a chin-high fastball.

Connor swung and missed.

Strike one.

"Too high!" Coach Hammond yelled.

Relax, Connor told himself. You're too anxious. Make him throw strikes.

Billy's next pitch was another fastball, shoulder-high this time. Connor couldn't lay off this one, either.

Strike two.

What are you doing? Connor thought, stepping out of the box to regroup. You're helping this guy, swinging at junk like that!

Out on the mound, Billy grinned. His confidence was back. He strutted around, glove tucked under one arm, rubbing the baseball with both hands.

Connor tapped the dirt from his spikes with the bat. He knew that every pitcher in the league considered it an accomplishment to strike him out. The last thing Connor wanted to do was give Billy an early Christmas present.

Connor took a couple of practice swings and stepped back in the box. He choked up on the bat and waved it menacingly, hands held high. Protect the plate, he told himself. Don't let the team down.

The noise from the stands was deafening now. Little

kids screamed and stomped on the bleachers. Mothers and fathers and aunts and uncles and grandparents were on their feet, clapping and cheering. Connor's parents weren't here, but they were in his head. *Can't let them down, either.*

Billy went into his windup. The pitch started low, a breaking ball, and Connor started his swing, even as the ball dropped wildly at the last second. He tried to check, but it was too late.

"Strike three!" the umpire yelled.

Billy let out a whoop and punched the sky.

Which is when something inside Connor snapped.

This time he smashed his batting helmet on the ground and waved a fist at Billy. Then he stomped back to the dugout and smacked a water bottle with his bat. The bottle exploded against one wall, just missing Marty's head.

"Coach, this is a warning!" the umpire shouted. "Any more of that, and he's gone!"

Coach Hammond nodded. He stood at the railing of the dugout, chewing furiously on his gum, and glared at Connor. "You need to cool off," he said quietly. He pointed to the end of the bench. "Take a seat—for the rest of the game."

Like last time, Connor's anger vanished in seconds. By the time he sat down, the first waves of remorse were already washing over him.

The chanting began seconds later.

It came from the Red Sox dugout, a loud, singsong noise that sounded like something from the crowd at the big international soccer matches he'd seen on TV.

"PSY-CHO SULL-EE!" went the chant. "PSY-CHO SULL-EE!"

Connor could feel the tears coming. He bent down and pretended to tie his spikes so no one could see his face.

But the chant continued, now even louder than before. "PSY-CHO SULL-EE! PSY-CHO SULL-EE!"

Somehow, he managed to cheer when Robbie Hammond, the next batter, doubled to left on a 3-and-2 count to drive in three runs.

Billy Burrell was so frustrated that he grabbed the front of his jersey and began growling and tearing at it with his teeth, something the Orioles had never seen before.

"And they're calling you psycho?" Marty Loopus said. "Get a load of Dog Boy out there."

But there was no cheering up Connor. He spent the rest of the game with a sick feeling in his stomach.

When it was over and the Orioles had won, 4–1, he lined up to slap hands with the other team. Billy smirked as he passed him. So did a few of the other Red Sox.

"Check the scoreboard, boys," Jordy said. "I'm pretty sure you guys lost."

"We'll see you again in the playoffs," Billy said. "Maybe Mr. Meltdown here can play the whole game this time."

Connor's face got hot. He wheeled to confront Billy, but Jordy quickly stepped between them.

"Better hope he doesn't play the whole game," Jordy told Billy. "That hit he got almost tore your head off."

Good ol' Jordy, Connor thought. Always the first to defend him.

But he still felt terrible. Out of the corner of his eye, he spotted a familiar figure with a camera bag walking toward him.

There was probably someone else in the entire world he wanted to see less than Melissa Morrow. But at the moment, he couldn't imagine who that could be.

"Quite a temper you have there, hotshot," she said.

"Don't start, Melissa," Connor said. "It's been a rough day."

Melissa smiled and watched the field empty as players and their parents headed to the parking lot. "Guess you heard the 'Psycho Sully' chant," she said.

"Kind of hard to miss," Connor said. He grabbed a water bottle and took a long drink, hoping it would soothe his stomach.

"Psycho Sully . . ." Melissa said. "Maybe that could be the headline on my story. Got some nice shots of you flipping out with your batting helmet, too."

Connor groaned. Now he was feeling absolutely nauseated. For a moment, he wondered if he'd get sick right there.

Knowing Melissa, she'd take photos of that, too. And print them in the *York Tattler*. Or even worse, post them on the Internet.

Only not before giving another lecture on the First Amendment.

The phone rang thirty minutes after he got home from the game, as he knew it would.

Connor looked at the caller ID screen: RAYMOND HAMMOND. Coach was not the sort of person who took long to address matters when they needed to be addressed. Connor knew this was one of the reasons why Coach had become a cop. When you see a thug knock down some poor old lady and run off with her purse, you don't stand there analyzing the situation. You take action. That was Coach.

Connor waited a few rings, hoping for a miracle.

Maybe there would be a sudden massive disruption of the telecommunications systems up and down the East Coast.

Maybe it would be caused by a solar flare, or the laser sabotage of a satellite in outer space by an evil madman intent on world domination, as he'd seen in an old James Bond movie.

Or maybe Coach's phone would suddenly burst into flames due to some horrible internal malfunction and be unusable for days.

Ha, fat chance! He finally picked up on the fifth ring.

"Connor?" Coach said. "It's got to stop, son."

"I know, Coach. I'm sorry."

"Two games in a row," Coach said.

"Yes, sir. I'm not proud of what I did."

"I wanted you to cool off before we talked."

"Thanks, Coach. I'm cool. It won't happen again."

There was silence on the other end.

Finally, Coach said: "This isn't like you. Anything bothering you, son? Everything okay at home, school, that sort of thing?"

"I'm fine, Coach."

"You know you can always talk to your mom and dad. They're good people. The best. You can always talk to me, too."

"I know. But everything's okay, honest."

The truth was, Connor didn't know anything. Two hours earlier, he was sure he had his temper under control, and then— Bam! He suddenly went psycho. Now his heart seemed to be beating wildly.

"Connor, we can't have any more of these blowups," Coach said. "You're running out of chances. Understand what I'm saying?"

"Absolutely, Coach."

"If it happens again, I'll have to take some action."

Take some action. There it was again. Oh, Coach would definitely take action, all right.

Connor hung up the phone. His stomach was in knots. Now he felt like he could hardly catch his breath.

Still in his Orioles uniform, he ran out the back door,

dropped to all fours in the cool grass, and began doing push-ups. Up-down, up-down, up-down . . . He wasn't keeping count, just banging them out as fast as he could, making them hurt, keeping his legs straight and his shoulders square, and dropping all the way until his chest brushed the grass.

It was twilight now. Upstairs, a light winked on in his parents' bedroom. It was his mom—she must have just come home from work.

Still, Connor didn't stop. Up-down, up-down, up down as he tried to block out thoughts. *Jerkwad . . . why'd I . . . wish I'd . . .* Ten more minutes, then twelve, then fifteen.

Finally, he slumped to the ground in exhaustion, his chest heaving, his shoulders aching, the sweat glistening on his face.

He felt better, he decided. But only in the way you'd feel better if someone was whacking you with a stick and they finally stopped.

Now there was no doubt: one more blowup, and Coach would kick him off the team. For good.

Three days later, the York Middle School cafeteria was even noisier than usual, with students talking excitedly, trays clattering, and a group of girls in one corner belting out the new Taylor Swift song as a teacher tried to shush them.

When Connor got to the lunch table, he found Jordy and Willie engaged in a favorite pastime: pretending to interview each other. The object was to cram in as many sports clichés as possible, just the way the major leaguers did when they were interviewed after a game. Jordy was using a plastic spoon as his fake microphone, and Willie was nodding earnestly with each answer.

"Willie, that was a breakout game for you against the Red Sox. . . ."

"Yeah, I'm seeing the ball real well, Jordy."

"Talk about that hit you had off Billy Burrell in the sixth inning."

"Well, I'm just trying to help the ballclub any way I can."

"You guys have a huge game coming up against the Yankees."

"Well, we play 'em one at a time, Jordy. But there's no quit in this team. We definitely plan to take care of business."

"What exactly does all that mean, Willie?"

"It is what it is, Jordy. I'm just happy to be here."

Connor laughed—it felt like the first time he had laughed in days. He opened a brown paper bag and pulled out the lunch his mom had packed: chicken sandwich, potato chips, apple, bottled water, and a half-dozen Oreos, the most perfect cookie known to humankind.

"Look who's here," Willie said. "Mr. Short Fuse himself."

"Mr. Ticking Time Bomb," Jordy added.

"Nope," Connor said, "I'm a new man. Mr. Calm. Mr. Cool." He tossed a couple of Oreos to Willie. "Here, you'll just bug me for these anyway."

Willie smiled and began happily devouring the cookies.

You want a kid to shut up, Connor thought, give him Oreos. Works every time.

Actually, Connor wasn't feeling like Mr. Calm at all—more like Mr. Stressed Out or Mr. Hair-on-Fire.

The night before, he had overheard his mom and dad talking in the kitchen. The conversation had started as a low murmur, but soon grew more animated, their voices rising. Apparently, this was about their monthly mortgage payment. Connor wasn't exactly sure what a monthly mortgage payment was. Something you paid to live where they lived? But as he stood at the top of the stairs, he could tell how worried they were.

"We could lose this house!" he'd heard his mom say.

"Karen, calm down," his dad had said. "No one's losing anything."

"Where are we supposed to get the money, Bill? Even with overtime, I'm not making enough to—"

"I have another job interview Wednesday," his dad had said. "And we still have some savings left. And, if worse comes to worst, we have Brianna's college fund. . . ."

"Which is supposed to be used for *college!*" his mom had shouted.

Connor didn't tell Brianna what he had overheard. She would have gone ballistic, and the last thing they needed right now was more tension in the house. But it was hard, keeping all these secrets. He looked at Jordy, who was polishing off a hamburger drenched in so much ketchup you couldn't see the meat. Why did Connor feel he had to hide the truth from his best friend? It wasn't like his dad was the only one looking for work. . . .

"So you're Mr. Calm now?" Jordy said.

"Yep," Connor said. "No more flipping out when things go wrong. I've found my inner peace." He closed his eyes and extended his arms with palms upraised, the pose of a blissed-out swami. "Ommmm," he intoned.

Jordy and Willie rolled their eyes.

"Give me a break," Jordy said.

"We'll see how long that inner peace stuff lasts," Willie said. "The next time the boy gets called out on a close play, he'll turn into an ax murderer."

Connor slid another Oreo across the table to Willie. Three cookies was a stiff price to pay to keep a kid off your back. But there were times it was worth it.

"You da man," Willie said with a grin.

"I'm serious, guys," Connor said. "Coach Hammond is

getting real tired of my act. I'm real tired of it, too."

"But it's such a charming part of your personality," Jordy said.

"Yeah," said Willie. "And who doesn't want a teammate known around the league as Psycho Sully?"

"Fine," Connor said. "Make your little jokes. But you'll see. I learned my lesson."

Connor didn't feel like regaling them with an account of his phone conversation with Coach Hammond. He was embarrassed enough without having anyone else know he was so close to getting thrown off the team.

The bell rang, signaling the end of lunch. The cafeteria was bedlam, with students dumping their trays, throwing away their trash, and shouting good-byes to each other as they hurried off to class.

"Just don't get tossed when we play the Yankees Friday," Jordy said when they were in the hall.

"Yeah, dude, we need you," Willie said, slapping him on the back. "No more crazy stuff."

"Ommmm," Connor said, smiling and doing his swami pose again.

But when his two buddies were gone, the frown returned to his face. Was there such a thing as a stressed-out swami? Because if so, he sure qualified.

Oh, he looked forward to playing the Yankees, just as he looked forward to every other baseball game he'd ever played in his life.

But with everything going on at home, he had to admit baseball wasn't quite as much fun anymore. He used to just worry about winning. Now he was worried about his parents, his house, his sister—not to mention getting through a game without exploding.

It made a guy want to go live in a cave, like a swami. No wonder they were so calm.

Eddie Murray Field was a shimmering green oasis in the center of town. It was a twenty-minute walk from Connor's house, or a seven-minute bike ride if he really pushed it, which meant weaving in between stroller-pushing moms and terrorizing slow-moving senior citizens on the sidewalks as he zipped by.

The town fathers kept the field lush and manicured. Before every game, an old man named Gus Papa would lovingly rake the red clay base paths, smooth the pitcher's mound, and line the batter's boxes until they gleamed in the afternoon sun.

Connor thought it was about the most perfect place on earth. In fact, on certain days, when there was a breeze and the smell of hot dogs and popcorn wafted from the tiny concession stand and mixed with the smell of new-mown grass, he wondered if it wasn't a little slice of heaven, too.

One day he had asked Mr. Papa why he took such meticulous care of the little field week in and week out. The old man had leaned on his rake and wiped the sweat from his eyes with a red handkerchief. "Well," he'd said finally, "all three of my boys played ball here. That was almost fifty years ago, long before it was named for Eddie. And this field was good to them. Baseball helped them grow into fine young men. Guess it's my humble way of giving back."

Connor wondered if baseball had been different fifty years ago. He wouldn't change anything about today. It was the Orioles versus the Yankees on this perfect field, on a perfect spring evening. About the only thing he'd change was not having his mom and dad in the stands. But his mom was working a double shift, and his dad was working on his résumé. Still, as he did every time he saw a baseball diamond, Connor could feel himself getting jacked up to play.

As usual, he was the first player to arrive. He jogged lightly across the outfield and then did some stretching, just the way the big leaguers did before a game at Camden Yards.

Soon players from both teams began trickling in. The Orioles gathered down the first-base line in front of their dugout and paired up to loosen their arms.

Willie spotted Connor and pointed an index finger at his own temple. "You're chill today, right?" he said.

"Mr. Calm," Connor said. He started to close his eyes and extend his palms, but Willie waved him off.

"Please," he said, "not the swami thing."

"Yeah, give that a rest, C," said Jordy, who was playing catch with Carlos Molina.

Connor smiled. "You're just jealous of my amazing new self-control," he said. "Derived from the ancient secrets of Hindu mystics."

"Now you sound like an infomercial," Willie said.

The first two innings went by like a heavyweight boxing match, both teams feeling each other out. The Yankees took a 3–0 lead in the third inning on two walks, an error in center field by Yancy Arroyo, and a double off Robbie Hammond, who struggled with his control.

But the Orioles started a comeback in the bottom of the inning. Joey Zinno, their catcher, led off with a sharp single to right.

Marty Loopus, making a rare start, followed with his usual weak bouncer to the pitcher for the first out.

"He's scared of me," Marty said upon returning to the dugout.

"The pitcher's scared of *you*?" Jordy said incredulously.

"Yep," Marty said. "Won't pitch to my power zone."

"You have a *power zone*?" Yancy said.

"Sure," Marty said. "Middle of the plate in. The whole league knows that."

"The *whole league* knows that?" Jordy said.

The rest of the Orioles smiled and shook their heads as Marty pulled off his batting gloves and got a drink of Gatorade.

Willie kept things going with a walk, Carlos drove in a run with a single, and Jordy doubled in two runs to tie the score.

The Orioles dugout was a sea of noise now. One out, one on, and who was marching to the plate but Connor Sullivan.

Standing in the third-base coaching box, Coach Hammond called time-out. He jogged down the line for a conference with Connor.

"Pitcher's getting tired," Coach said. "Wait for your pitch and drive it."

Connor nodded and walked back to the batter's box. He knew that was Coach's way of saying: permission granted to swing for the fences.

Usually, Coach Hammond didn't want his players trying to hit home runs. It changed their swings, he said. Instead of a short, compact swing—the ideal—they'd develop a long, slow swing, trying to jack the ball out of the park. "Don't worry about where it goes," Coach always told them. "Just hit the ball somewhere. And hit it hard."

On occasion, though, Coach would make an exception for Connor, who had a sweet swing and didn't try to kill the ball. This obviously was one of those occasions.

Connor dug in against the Yankees pitcher, a kid named Georgie Rosario, who happened to be in his guitar class.

He fouled off a pitch, then looked at three outside pitches without moving the bat off his shoulder. He was waiting for his pitch. Three and one count. This isn't rocket science, Connor thought. Georgie has to throw a strike now.

Georgie did. It was a belt-high fastball with not much on it. Connor turned on it perfectly and hit a long, soaring blast over the fence in left field.

Just like that, it was 5–3 Orioles. As their dugout exploded, Connor went into his home run trot and high-fived Coach Hammond as he rounded third base.

"Sure!" said Marty, standing on the top step of the dugout with arms outstretched in exasperation. "They'll pitch to *his* power zone!"

In the dugout, Connor happily accepted fist-bumps and backslaps from the rest of the Orioles. Not bad so far, he thought. Just keep your cool the rest of the way.

The Orioles were still clinging to a two-run lead in the fifth inning when the Yankees came to bat.

Mike Cutko came on in relief of Robbie and promptly walked the first two batters, then struck out the next two. Next up was the Yankees dangerous cleanup hitter, Jake Hiaasen.

Jake was a big kid, too—not as tall as Connor, but bigger in the chest and shoulders. During football season, he was a star running back for the Dulaney Jets, with a reputation for flattening would-be tacklers, whose eyes tended to widen when they saw Jake steaming toward them.

"Everybody back!" Coach Hammond yelled, motioning to his outfielders.

Marty was already so far back in right field he looked to be in a different zip code. Now he backed up even farther, until he was practically leaning against the fence.

Mike's first two pitches were in the dirt, and Jake held up on both. The next was a fastball at the knees. Jake took a mighty cut, but topped the ball, hitting a slow bouncer to short.

Connor charged it and scooped the ball with two hands. The runners on first and second had gotten a nice jump, so Connor knew his only play was at first.

He planted his left foot and threw off-balance—and watched in horror as the ball sailed high over Jordy's head, bouncing against the chain-link fence and rolling down the right-field line as two runs scored.

Now it was 5–5.

What happened next felt like a dream—or maybe more like a nightmare. *Don't do it!* he told himself, but already he was screaming "*No-o-o!*" and tearing the glove off his left hand and sailing it high in the air over Willie's head.

In a flash, the umpire bolted from behind home plate and tore off his mask. Pointing at Connor, he yelled, "That's it, son! You're outta here!"

Stomping across the first-base line, Connor snarled at Jordy: "You couldn't jump any higher for that throw? My grandma could've caught that!"

Jordy's shocked expression just made Connor angrier. Reaching the dugout, he picked up a bat and fired it angrily against the wall. It ricocheted and hit Robbie in the knee, but Robbie was too stunned to cry out in pain.

"CONNOR!" Coach Hammond barked. "That's enough! Get your stuff and go home. I'll call you in the morning."

But Connor didn't care about his bat or his glove or his equipment bag right now. He didn't care about baseball, either. Like the ump said, he was outta there.

As he bolted from the dugout and ran to his bike, he could feel the tears coming. And this time there was no holding them back.

This time he had really screwed up.

Connor fed four tokens into the batting machine and picked up his thirty-one-inch Rawlings bat. He took his usual stance: slightly open, close to the plate, feet shoulder-width apart, weight balanced—and waited for the silver arm to uncoil and snap forward with the pitch.

It was quiet inside the cavernous Sports arcade, especially for a Saturday afternoon. A few kids and their parents played mini-golf, and three bored-looking teenagers were winning at Skee-Ball, collecting fistfuls of red tickets to exchange for fistfuls of cheap trinkets. Only one other batting cage was occupied, with a chubby little kid, maybe ten years old, getting tips from his dad—if you could call them tips.

"Level swing!" the dad barked. "Don't be afraid of the ball! No! Step into the pitch!"

Connor shook his head sadly. Over the years he'd seen lots of kids quit baseball because their moms and dads pressured them and over-instructed them and took all the fun out of the game. This kid looked so nervous, he was probably dreaming about swim team tryouts already.

"Get that bat ready!" the dad shouted as the kid whiffed on yet another cut. "No, too slow! Try it again!"

Hoo boy, Connor thought. Bet the kid wishes Dad was on a nice long out-of-town business trip about now.

The fact that Sports was nearly empty suited Connor just fine. Right now he was focusing on what a mess he'd made of his life just twenty-four hours earlier. The way he saw it, his latest stupid blowup had succeeded in causing four disastrous consequences:

1. After Connor left, the Orioles had gone on to lose to the Yankees, 8–5. It was their first loss of the season. And if anyone was voting on the goat of the game, Connor knew he'd win it hands down. In fact, he could almost feel the horns growing out of his head right now.

2. In a brief phone call earlier that morning, Coach Hammond had informed Connor that his ejection from the Yankee game also carried with it an automatic one-game suspension from the league. Which meant the Orioles would be without him when they faced the Tigers next week, potentially setting the stage for— ta-da!—their second loss of the season. And that was assuming Coach hadn't already kicked him off the team and was just waiting for the right time to tell him.

3. He had succeeded in seriously hurting the feelings of his best friend in the whole world, Jordy Marsh.

Connor wondered if he would ever get over the look on Jordy's face after he had snarled and accused him of not jumping high enough for that terrible throw. Jordy had looked like a friendly golden retriever that had just been bopped on the nose with a rolled-up newspaper for no reason.

4. His latest eruption and ejection had been observed and captured in its full glove-tossing, bat-throwing, crybaby glory by one Melissa Morrow, who was probably feeding a video clip of the whole thing to YouTube right now and planning a headline in the *York Tattler* that read: "Youth Baseball Star Really *Is* Nuts!"

Connor could imagine the photo spread that would accompany that story, too. It would be a montage of all his on-field eruptions that would eventually be posted on Facebook, so that young ballplayers all over the world could comment and make fun of him.

"Justin, do you want to get better or not?!" the chubby kid's dad yelled now. "Then let's go! Take a good hack at it!"

Connor tried to block out the dad's ridiculous instructions. It reminded him how lucky he was to have a dad who was patient and made learning baseball fun.

Before he lost his job, Bill Sullivan had always come with Connor to these Saturday batting sessions. Connor missed having him at the back of the cage, quietly offering tips. Now that his dad was spending so much time looking for work, he hadn't come to Sports in weeks.

Connor was working on hitting curveballs today—this was one of the few places that had a pitching machine that threw breaking balls. He held his hands high, moving the bat in small circles, trying for a sense of rhythm and timing and the short, compact swing Coach Hammond recommended for his players.

Of course, that was assuming he still *was* one of Coach's players. The odds were great that that was no longer the case. Coach was a patient man. But how many of Connor's crazy tantrums could he reasonably be expected to endure?

And who knew if any of Connor's Orioles teammates wanted him back, either? He'd seen the embarrassed looks on their faces when he'd slammed the glove down, stomped back to the dugout, and thrown the bat, accidentally hitting Robbie. And they were definitely ticked at the way he'd exploded at Jordy.

After hitting some fifty balls in the cage and concentrating on driving the ball to all fields, Connor's whole body was tired. Unfortunately, the chubby kid was still being tortured by his dad. The dad had jumped in the cage now and was demonstrating possibly the ugliest baseball swing Connor had ever seen. He looked like a man trying to beat a snake off a tree branch with a hoe. Justin, the chubby kid, was trying hard not to laugh. So was Connor.

Now Justin was taking some cuts, but still without much luck. Finally the dad gave up in disgust.

"I'll wait for you in the car," he said with a wave of his hand as he stormed out.

Connor watched the boy throw the bat down and slump dejectedly in a chair.

He walked over and said gently, "Hey, Justin."

The boy looked up warily.

"You don't know me—my name's Connor. I overheard your dad. . . ."

Justin didn't answer; but his face said it all: he was mortified.

"I was wondering . . ." Connor went on. "Could I show you something that might help? My treat."

Justin just sat there, watching suspiciously as Connor fed some tokens into the batting machine and borrowed the boy's bat.

"Keep your head still when you swing," Connor said, taking his stance as the machine whirred to life. "You're doing this." He took a big cut and missed, pulling his head off the ball with an exaggerated motion.

Justin winced.

"Hey, don't worry about it—you're still learning. I just don't agree with your dad's teaching technique." Connor chuckled a little, and Justin cracked a smile.

"What you want to do is this," Connor continued. This time he kept his head still and his eyes locked on the ball and hit a sharp line drive. "Now you try it."

The boy hesitated a moment, then took the bat and got in his stance.

He did as Connor instructed and, after a couple of misses, hit a shot up the middle. His eyes widened and he turned to Connor, laughing with delight.

"Try it again," Connor said. And again the boy hit it solidly, a shot to left field.

"Wow!" the kid said. "Thanks."

"No problem. Keep it up, and you'll give your dad the surprise of his life."

Justin nodded, his face beaming.

My work here is done, Connor thought. Why can't everything in life be this easy to fix?

Justin was now happily taking more swings, so Connor went off to buy a drink from the vending machine. Helping the kid had taken his mind off his own troubles for a few minutes. But now he was back to full-time brooding.

He'd been too ashamed that morning to tell his mom and dad about his latest blowup with the Orioles—not that they would have had time to listen.

His mom had gone off to work early, saying all the ER nurses were taking a special training course that would probably last up until her regular work shift. And his dad had left right after, bound for a job interview with a car dealership on the other side of town.

Brianna had been home. She'd even gotten out of bed before her customary Saturday rise-and-shine time of noon. But this wasn't the kind of thing you talked over with your big sister.

Connor knew how she would react: a dramatic shake of her head, the requisite rolling of her eyes, followed by her standard advice to "just grow up!"

So Connor had spent a sleepless night and now an anxious day with dozens of questions running through his head. Why did he keep losing his temper? It was getting scary now, this feeling that he couldn't control himself whenever he screwed up on the ball field.

What was Coach going to do? Would he give him one

more chance? Or was he just waiting for him to chill for a day or two before dropping the hammer and kicking him off the team?

Connor couldn't imagine a spring without baseball, the game he had loved since he was a little kid. He couldn't imagine the Orioles going to the championship game— they were 12–1 now, almost sure to make it—and him not being a part of it.

Draining the last of his Snapple, he stared out the window. The sky was as gray as dishwater. Low clouds hung as far as the eye could see, and a steady rain had begun to fall. The ride home on his bike would be a wet one.

A thought popped into his head, and he smiled ruefully: *Maybe I'll catch pneumonia and not have to worry about baseball for a while.*

Then he caught himself and shook his head softly.

Nah, I don't have that kind of luck.

It was a gorgeous spring day, the dreary rain of twenty-four hours earlier having given way to a dazzling blue sky and white puffy clouds that looked low enough to touch. Connor and his dad were outside painting the garage door when the black Ford pickup roared up the driveway, spraying gravel in all directions.

Connor took in the polished chrome, the fog lights, the Yosemite Sam "Back Off!" mud flaps, and the burly figure in sunglasses behind the wheel and instantly arrived at a conclusion: *My life is over.*

The driver's-side door opened, and out stepped Coach Hammond. Connor saw that Coach had ditched his usual Windbreaker and khaki pants for his snappy off-duty cop look: baseball cap, polo shirt, jeans with a big, silver belt buckle, and snakeskin cowboy boots.

"Hi, guys," Coach said cheerfully. "What's going on here, a little father-son bonding project?"

"Hi, Ray," his dad said. He glanced over at Connor. "Sunday afternoon, and my son's baseball coach is visiting us instead of keeping America safe. This can't be good."

Connor could feel his heart race. His hands were starting to sweat, too.

Coach smiled broadly and clapped him on the shoulder. "Hey, buddy," he said, "think I could talk to your dad alone for a few minutes?"

Connor nodded blankly. He laid his paintbrush atop the can of white exterior latex at his feet and wiped his hands with a rag as the two men went inside. Then, feeling like he was moving in slow motion, he went into the backyard, picked up his glove, and began mindlessly firing balls at the bounce-back net.

Okay, he thought, I'm definitely getting kicked off the Orioles. Coach didn't drive all the way over here to talk about the weather. Or about all the bad guys he's tossed in the slammer.

No, Coach would come right to the point with his dad: "Bill, your son's a head case. A certified nut job. His melt-downs are killing the team. I have to cut him loose."

Five minutes went by, then ten, then fifteen. Connor could feel himself getting more and more anxious as he took ground balls off the bounce-back, then line drives, then fly balls.

From time to time, he stole a glance at the sliding glass door and saw the two men sitting at the kitchen table, talking. Actually, Coach was doing all the talking. His dad was doing all the listening, occasionally shaking his head.

Connor groaned inwardly. That head-shaking was not a good sign. He could almost see tiny puffs of steam coming out of his dad's ears, like in Road Runner cartoons, when Wile E. Coyote was outsmarted by that crazy bird.

More time went by. The waiting was killing Connor now.

He thought back to a movie he'd seen a few weeks ear-lier. It was about an English nobleman in the nineteenth century who was falsely accused of a crime and thrown into a dungeon, where he spent hours wondering if they were going to hang him or shove him in front of a firing squad. Connor could relate to the feeling. The English nobleman eventually escaped, but there didn't appear to be any way out of this mess for Connor.

Finally, the sliding glass door opened and his dad shouted: "Connor, come on in here."

Connor fired one more ball against the bounce-back and jogged to the back door. Then he slowed and thought: *Why am I hustling? Who rushes to his own execution?*

When he got to the kitchen table, his dad and Coach Hammond had big mugs of coffee in front of them. Both men looked grim as Connor took a seat. No one said any-thing for a few seconds.

Finally his dad cleared his throat. "Ray filled me in on your latest temper tantrums. And the league suspension."

Connor started to say something in his own defense, but Coach held up his hand. "I didn't come here to snitch, Connor," Coach said. "That wasn't my intention."

Connor nodded, immediately thinking, Here it comes. Bye-bye baseball. The room suddenly seemed very still. Very warm, too.

"I'm disappointed in you, son," his dad said. "Didn't we just talk about this the other day?"

Connor's mouth was so dry, he felt like reaching over and taking a swig of his dad's coffee. But he'd probably end up spitting it across the table, like a sitcom character who'd tasted something weird. And that wouldn't exactly earn him any points with the two men.

"Coach seems to feel there's something bothering you," his dad said in a gentler tone. "I told him things have been a little tense around here. So you didn't tell Coach I lost my job?"

Connor shook his head.

"Well, he knows now," his dad continued. "I never wanted that to be a big secret. Like I told you: Lots of people have lost jobs in this economy. It's nothing to be ashamed of."

Connor looked at Coach, who nodded in agreement.

"Is that what's been bothering you, buddy?" his dad said. "You never lost your temper like this before. Your mom and I were so proud of how you—"

Connor couldn't hold back any longer. Now it all came pouring out: how scared he was that his dad might not find another job; how there never seemed to be enough money to do the fun things they used to do as a family; how worried his mom and Brianna were all the time; how the news on TV was always about the high unemployment rate; how Dana Petrillo's dad had been out of work a year now and still couldn't find anything. . . .

His dad came around the table and wrapped his arms around him, but still Connor couldn't stop, he'd been carrying this inside for so long.

"I heard . . . when the two of you were talking the other night . . . Mom said we could lose the house," he said through tears. "I don't want . . . I needed something to go right . . . and when I messed up, I got so mad. . . ."

"It's all right, buddy," his dad said, rocking him gently. "We're not losing this house—or anything else."

Connor didn't know how long he sat there blubbering. A minute? Two? Finally he straightened up and wiped his eyes with the back of his hand. He was embarrassed to have Coach see him cry. Although, what difference did it make now? Coach would probably never want to see him again, anyway.

"Connor, can I tell you something?" Coach said now in a soft voice. "I know exactly what you're going through. Your dad, too. See, I was laid off once. Years ago, before I became a crime-fighting superhero."

Connor managed a weak smile as he tried to imagine Coach in your basic superhero costume: tights, knee-high boots, cape, maybe a mask. It wasn't a pretty picture.

"One minute I'm a truck driver for a parcel delivery service," Coach continued; "the next minute the boss is handing me a severance check and saying, 'Don't bother coming in Monday.' Robbie and his sister Jackie were babies at the time. Mary was pregnant with Ashley."

Connor was hanging on every word now, fascinated to learn that Coach had ever been anything but a cop.

"At first you think it's the end of the world," Coach said. "But it's not. You have to tighten your belt for a while, go without a few things, but you also have to stay optimistic. Nasty surprises like this have a way of turning out for the best. Look at me—if it hadn't happened, I wouldn't have joined the police force. Your dad's a good man. He won't be out of work much longer."

"Got two interviews lined up right now," his dad said, patting Connor's arm. "And both are promising."

Connor was starting to feel better. Just talking about this after so many months was a relief. Then he looked at Coach and felt his spirits sag. What would he do without baseball, the game he lived for, the best game in the whole world?

Coach seemed to be reading his mind. "You want to know if I'm kicking you off the Orioles." He propped his elbows on the table and steepled his fingers. "To be honest, I thought seriously about doing just that. But I wanted to talk to your dad first, see what was going on. And I'm glad I did."

He leaned forward. "Connor, you and your family are going through a rough time. But losing your temper on the baseball field won't make things better at home—you know that, right?"

Connor just hung his head, afraid to hear more.

"You've been under a lot of stress. It explains why you haven't been yourself lately. So I'm willing to give you another chance."

"Yes!" Connor said, jumping up. He let out a whoop. "Thanks, Coach!"

Coach quickly held up both hands. "But here's the deal," he said. "One more blowup, and you're off the team for good. And next time there'll be no discussion about it. Understand?"

Connor nodded happily and looked at his dad, who was smiling now.

"First thing you have to do is apologize to your

teammates, especially Jordy," Coach said. "But I have a feeling you'll be just fine from now on." He stood and took his coffee mug over to the sink. Then he smiled.

"Now, if you gentlemen will excuse me," he said, "I'm off to work. Bet the bad guys are quaking in fear already."

While Connor's dad walked Coach to the door, Connor slumped forward and put his head down on the table. He couldn't remember ever feeling so tired—or so relieved.

Coach was giving him one more chance. This time he really couldn't blow it.

The Connor Sullivan Apology Tour—

Connor even thought about having T-shirts made up, orange and black, for every kid on the Orioles—began with a visit to Jordy Marsh the next day after school.

Jordy lived in a big, rambling Colonial not far from Eddie Murray Field. The house was ringed by a white picket fence that was patrolled endlessly by a hyper sheepdog named Rex. Jordy's dad called him Rex the Wonder Dog, after a comic-book hero that fought crime and rooted out Nazi spies. Connor thought Rex was too dumb to root out anything except maybe an old tennis ball from under the porch. But Connor had to admit that Rex was impressive as a watchdog. He could hear you coming a mile away, no matter what side of the perimeter he was sniffing around at that particular moment.

Sure enough, as soon as Connor opened the front gate, Rex came tearing around the corner, barking like a demon.

"You've still got it, Rex," Connor said, patting him on the head and setting off a frenzy of tail-wagging. "Still the unanimous choice for Guard Dog of the Year."

The commotion caused Jordy's mom to stick her head out an upstairs window.

"Oh, hi, Connor," she said. "Jordy's around back somewhere."

Connor found Jordy shooting baskets at the portable hoop his parents had given him last Christmas. He could feel himself tense up, wondering what kind of greeting he'd get from his old friend.

Or maybe *ex*-friend was the better word now.

"Well, if it isn't Mr. Anger Management himself," Jordy said.

"Ohhhh-kay," Connor said. "Guess that answers that."

Jordy's eyes narrowed with suspicion. "Answers what?"

"Whether you're still mad at me."

"Me?" Jordy said with a snort. "Why should I be mad?" He took a jump shot that clanged off the back of the rim. "Let's see," he said, chasing down the rebound. "First, you airmail a throw over my head in a big game. Then, when I can't catch it—and Yao Ming couldn't have caught that throw if he jumped on a trampoline—you yell at me for not trying."

Connor felt his face redden.

Jordy took another shot from the foul line. This one grazed the front of the rim and bounced back to him. "So you have another of your stupid temper tantrums," he went on, "and we lose our first game of the season because we're missing our best player."

Connor opened his mouth to speak, but Jordy wasn't finished.

"Now you're suspended for the Tigers game. And

guess what? If we lose that, we're no lock to play for the championship."

He took a jump shot from the corner that swished through the net, then turned and looked directly at Connor. "This might be a news flash to you, but you've been acting like a real jerk."

Connor hung his head and kicked at some loose gravel, searching for something to say.

He and Jordy had been best friends since third grade. But he'd never seen his bud this angry—not that it wasn't for good reason.

Neither boy spoke for several seconds.

Finally, Connor took a deep breath and said, "You're right. I've been a jackass. I came here to say I'm sorry."

Now it was Jordy who seemed uncomfortable.

"Well, maybe 'jackass' is a little strong. . . ." he said, trying to lighten the mood.

"No, it's the right word," Connor said softly. "My dad's been laid off. I haven't handled it real well."

He gave Jordy a CliffsNotes version of what his family had been going through, complete with the admission that all the worry had turned him into a walking powder keg on the baseball field.

When he was done, Jordy shook his head. "Dude," he said, "why didn't you tell me earlier?"

Connor shrugged. "Too embarrassed, I guess."

"You *are* a jackass," Jordy said with a smile. Then he got serious again. "But, um, how do we know you're not going to freak out again? I mean, you've been like Jekyll and Hyde."

"I had a long talk with my dad and Coach yesterday. We hashed it all out." Connor didn't mention the crying part. "It helped a lot, and I feel better now."

Jordy looked at him warily. "You sure? Because here's something that might make you feel worse again."

Connor sighed and sat down in the grass. "Okay. Lay it on me."

"It's about Melissa Morrow."

Connor put his head in his hands. He knew what was coming next. It was like knowing how a movie was going to end before you actually saw it.

"I ran into her after school today, and she showed me a video on her camcorder. It shows your meltdown in the Yankees game," Jordy said.

Connor groaned.

"She's thinking about putting it on the *Tattler*'s Web site, along with a story: 'Are Young Athletes Under Too Much Pressure to Succeed?' Don't take this the wrong way, but it's an awesome video!"

"Great," Connor said dryly. "Glad it was entertaining."

"Oh, it was," Jordy said. "One minute you're Bruce Banner. The next minute you turn into the Hulk."

Connor tried to imagine himself going into such a rage that he morphed into a beetle-browed freak with a thickly-muscled green body who could toss cars around like they were matchboxes. Actually, his tantrums almost felt like that—well, without the benefit of superhuman strength. If he had that, at least his homers would go for miles. . . .

"The video lasts for, like, two minutes," Jordy continued. "The camera's on you from the minute you sail that lame throw over my head—sorry—until you leave the field crying."

"She got that too, huh?" Connor said, feeling worse by the minute.

Jordy nodded.

"Yeah, she must have some super-zoom on that camera, too, because she even caught you throwing the bat in the dugout. The one that almost kneecapped Robbie?"

"No need for the blow-by-blow," Connor said, holding up one hand. "I was there, remember?"

"But here's the strange part," Jordy said. "She kept filming even after you left. And she kept the camera on one of our esteemed teammates. You'll never guess which one. Okay, here's a hint: his initials are M.L."

"NO O O!" Connor said.

"Yes! Marty Loopus!" Jordy said.

"But why?"

"Don't know. But the video has two minutes of you going thermonuclear, right? Then it has two minutes of Marty at shortstop not doing anything except swirling dirt with his spikes and blowing bubbles and swatting at a couple of butterflies. It's really hysterical."

"What's the headline there?" Connor said. "'Are Young Athletes Too Bored to Succeed?'"

By now both of them were laughing.

"Actually, I have to hand it to Marty," said Connor. "He's always a good sport. Unlike me. I have to apologize to him, and the whole team. And I have to try to stop Melissa." He stood up to leave.

Just then Rex the Wonder Dog shot past them in a

blur. They watched as he chased a squirrel that quickly scampered up a tree, leaving poor Rex howling in frustration.

Nazi spies? Connor thought. Yeah, right. The dog has a nervous breakdown just tracking tiny woodland creatures.

"Forget Melissa," Jordy said, tossing Connor the basketball. "A little one-on-one? Game to eleven? Winner gets the other guy's cookies at lunch tomorrow?"

Connor grinned. "Prepare to be dominated," he said. "And make sure your mom packs Oreos after your beat-down."

He dribbled to the top of the key and launched a pretty jump shot over Jordy's outstretched arm. It swished through the net. "This'll be even easier than I thought!" Connor crowed.

Jordy was right—he'd worry about Melissa later. Right now he was playing hoops in the warm sunshine with his best friend, and a pack of Oreos, America's finest cookie, was on the line.

He hadn't felt this happy in days.

Connor tried to remember the last time he was a spectator at Eddie Murray Field instead of a ballplayer. Maybe it was back when he was five years old, when his dad would take him to watch the older kids play. The two of them would hang out behind the backstop, Connor perched on his dad's shoulders, his dad calling out what kind of pitch had just been thrown and asking him whether it was a ball or strike.

Back then he'd felt on top of the world. Today, as the Orioles prepared to face the Tigers and he prepared to sit in the stands with a big, fat suspension, he felt like the world's biggest loser.

Wait, wasn't there a reality show called *The Biggest Loser*? That was about people trying to lose weight. If they ever came up with a show about wacko young ballplayers with anger issues, Connor was sure they'd call him. They'd probably send a limo to pick him up the same day.

He walked over to the sidelines, where the Orioles were warming up, and Coach Hammond was filling out the lineup card. Everyone seemed happy to see him, which made him feel better. He gathered the team around him and quickly apologized for his meltdowns.

"Yo, Connor," said Willie Pitts. "When you do the mass apology thing, you have to say 'I apologize to anyone whom I might have offended.'" Willie put his hand over his heart and looked reverent. "That's what all the politicians and pro athletes and movie stars do."

"Yeah," said Jordy. "And when you're done, you have to look at the audience and say: 'I will not be taking any questions. My family and I ask that you respect our privacy during this difficult time.'"

Everyone laughed, including Coach Hammond. Connor looked down sheepishly. But he had to admit Willie and Jordan were right—that was how all those big-shot public apologies sounded. Totally insincere.

Just last week, another major league ballplayer, Los Angeles Dodgers slugger Dean (Dream) Sanders, had tested positive for steroids and been slapped with a three-month suspension. And during a nationally televised news conference a few days later, a tearful Sanders had essentially mouthed—almost word for word—the same platitudes Willie and Jordy had just uttered.

As the laughter died down, Marty Loopus walked up to Connor, put both hands on his shoulders, and looked him squarely in the eye. "Playoffs start next week," he said solemnly. "Promise us you'll control that famous temper of yours? Or do I have to keep carrying this team by myself?"

Now the rest of the Orioles hooted and laughed and smacked Marty with their caps as a grinning Connor held up his hand and said: "I promise, I promise!"

Finally Coach Hammond shouted: "Game starts in five minutes, gentlemen!" and the Orioles went back to their warm-ups.

League rules dictated that suspended players couldn't sit in the dugout with their team during a game, so Connor took a seat in the stands, which were already filling up.

Jordy's mom smiled and waved as he climbed the bleachers. So did Mr. and Mrs. Molina, Gabe's parents; and Mr. Pitts, Willie's dad. Mr. Zinno, Joey's dad, who never said a word to anyone at these games, even came over, shook his hand, and said, "Gonna miss you out there, champ. Need you back in the lineup."

But there was something else about the way the parents looked at him. Was that pity he saw in their eyes? Or were they saying a little prayer to themselves: *Thank God that spoiled brat isn't my kid*? Might as well be wearing a sign around my neck that says HEAD CASE, Connor thought, his mood darkening again.

For once he was glad not to have his own parents here. Wouldn't they be proud, watching their boy sit out for disciplinary reasons!

As the Orioles took the field, Connor saw something else that didn't improve his mood. Melissa Morrow, red hair swinging in a ponytail underneath a baseball cap, was clambering up the steps toward him.

Instantly he felt a throbbing in his forehead.

"The great Connor Sullivan! Thought I'd find you here," she said, plopping her backpack down next to him. "This is the game you sit out, right? For going nuts against the Yankees?"

That's Melissa for you, Connor thought. As subtle as a punch in the mouth.

"We need to talk," he said.

"Not a problem," Melissa said, pulling out a camera and notebook. "But it'll have to be after the game. Just 'cause you're not playing doesn't mean I'm not working."

Quickly, she changed lenses on her camera, looped it around her neck, and went clattering back down the bleachers. For a moment, Connor fantasized about reaching into the backpack she left behind, pulling out Melissa's camcorder, and deleting his big meltdown. No, he was too chicken. Besides, with his luck, he'd probably be arrested.

That would be a nice phone conversation to have with his parents: "Mom, Dad, I'm in jail. How're we fixed for bail money?"

When she reached the bottom of the bleachers, Melissa turned, pointed the camera up at him, and began clicking away.

Great, Connor thought. I can see the photo caption now: "Hothead ballplayer serves well-deserved suspension. Did this dope finally learn his lesson?"

When she finished, she smiled, gave him the thumbs-up sign, and walked down the first-base line to shoot game action.

And there was plenty of that—unfortunately, not the kind the Orioles wanted to see.

Mike Cutko, their number two pitcher, made it through the first two innings without incident. But he gave up two runs in the third on a mammoth home run by Deon Mobley, the Tigers catcher, and two more in the fifth on two errors, a walk, and a double.

Meanwhile, the Orioles bats were quiet. No, they were more than quiet—they were practically comatose.

Jordy singled in the third inning, and Marty Loopus reached on a slow roller to second that the Tiger second baseman managed to trip over. Somehow it was ruled a hit by the official scorer, prompting Marty to do the kind of celebratory dance normally reserved for a walk-off homer. And that was it for the Orioles offense.

You know you're in trouble when Marty Loopus is your second-leading hitter, Connor thought.

He cheered hard for his team the whole game, even though it felt weird to be clapping from the sidelines instead of in the thick of the action. But the final score was Tigers 5, Orioles 0. The Orioles had lost their second game of the season, which made him feel guilty and even more like a loser.

The Orioles were still going to the playoffs—both the Yankees and Red Sox had lost a day earlier, which meant both teams had two losses, too. But now there was no margin for error. One more loss, and the O's' season would be over, thanks to a certain star shortstop who couldn't control his emotions.

As the two teams slapped hands, Connor grabbed Melissa's backpack and hurried down to the field. He found her over by the Orioles dugout, taking photos of Marty Loopus in his batting stance as Marty recounted, with great enthusiasm and detail, his titanic roller to second base.

"Connor!" Marty said when he spotted him. "Was I all over that pitch, or what?"

"You *owned* that guy, Marty," Connor said. "Now, uh, could you excuse us for a moment?"

He took Melissa by the elbow and steered her to a spot a few feet away.

"What's up, hotshot?" she said. "Oh, that's right, you wanted to talk."

Connor lowered his voice, not wanting the entire Orioles team, as well as parents, siblings, groundskeepers, and the folks who ran the concession stand to listen in.

"I understand you have a video of my, um, unfortunate behavior against the Yankees," he began.

"Sure do," Melissa said. "It's a beauty, too. A classic study of anger and frustration, captured in astonishing detail."

"You make it sound like it's up for an Oscar," Connor said.

Melissa beamed and nodded. "It's some of my best work as a photojournalist," she said.

"Well, that's . . . *great*, Melissa. But you're not really, uh, putting it on the school's Web site tonight?"

"Oh, no," Melissa said. "I couldn't do that."

Connor breathed a huge sigh of relief.

"But it'll be up there first thing tomorrow," Melissa said. "Soon as I get to school."

"*What?!*" Connor said. "But you can't . . . !"

Melissa rolled her eyes and shook her head, letting Connor know her infinite supply of patience was being sorely tested. "Remember the little chat we had about the First Amendment? Do we have to go over that again?"

"No, it's not that. . . ." Connor said. He groped for the right words. "Look, I'm not a young athlete feeling too much pressure to succeed, or whatever you're writing. I'm just a kid dealing with a family thing. And I . . . I let it get to me."

"You sure do blow up nicely for the camera," Melissa said.

It was a struggle for Connor to keep himself from blowing up right then. He took a deep breath and tried not to talk through gritted teeth. "But I'm better now, honest," he said. Was his voice getting whiny? He couldn't be sure. "It's not going to happen again. At least give me a chance to prove it."

"That'd be good for you, but what's in it for me?" Melissa said. "I'd be left without a story."

"What about the story you were going to write before? You know, the big profile? 'Inquiring minds want to know,' and all that?"

"That was before you got really interesting," she said. "Anger issues are so fascinating. Don't you agree?"

Connor felt himself blush. Or flush with anger—he wasn't sure which.

"Look," he said, "you can interview me for as long as you want."

"How generous of you," she said dryly. She took her backpack from him and carefully placed her camera and notebook inside. Then she zipped it up and slipped both arms through the loops.

"So, do we have a deal?" Connor asked hopefully.

"I'll think about it," she said.

"Oh, come on!" Connor said. "Give me a break!"

"Uh-uh," Melissa said, wagging her finger. "Temper,

temper." She started to walk away, leaving him standing there, slack-jawed.

Then she turned to deliver one last zinger. "You know something, Connor? You're cute when you're stressed."

Then I must be a real knockout, Connor thought, because I'm majorly stressed right now.

Billy Burrell's default expression

was a smirk.

Once in a while, he could manage something that almost resembled a smile, especially when he was kissing up to teachers and parents, or trying to impress girls. But for the most part, Billy walked around looking as if he knew something you didn't, because he was so smart and you were so dumb.

When Connor ran into him in the hall at York Middle the day after the Orioles–Tigers game, Billy was wearing his A-1 smirk. He was also accompanied by two of his semi-thuggish Red Sox teammates—Connor recognized both as instigators of the "Psycho Sully" chant of a couple weeks ago.

As always, Billy dispensed with the usual pleasantries. "We're going to kill you guys in the playoffs," he said.

"Don't keep stuff inside, Billy," Connor said. "Tell us what you really think."

Connor was in a good mood, having just come from the computer lab, where, with his heart hammering in his chest, he had checked the *Tattler*'s Web site to see if he was a featured attraction.

There was a story about the new science wing opening, and a piece about Ms. Peggy Jackman, who was retiring after thirty years of teaching English. There was a column titled "No Wonder Johnny's Enormous!" that decried the lack of nutritious food selections in the cafeteria, and another titled "Down with the Fashion Police!" advocating that students be allowed to wear T-shirts with political slogans to school.

But there was no story or video, thank goodness, about a head case twelve-year-old ballplayer under too much pressure to succeed.

Connor had been so relieved that he'd actually lowered his head onto the keyboard and whispered, "Thank you, Melissa," before signing off.

Now here were Billy and his two creepy teammates, Kyle something and Marcus something, getting in his face about the playoffs. Any other time, he would have been irritated just by the sight of them.

But today he was so thankful to not be an Internet laughingstock that he found talking to Billy to be almost, well, tolerable.

Except now Billy was taunting him, getting right in his grille.

"You plan to play the whole game this time, Psycho Sully?" he said. Then he grinned and elbowed Kyle and Marcus, who promptly started laughing as if this were the funniest thing they had ever heard.

"Yeah, I think so," Connor said. "Hope you throw that

same pitch you did last time. Remember? The one I tattooed over your head?"

Billy's grin disappeared, replaced by a scowl, his second-favorite facial expression. Seeing Billy's, Kyle and Marcus felt compelled to break out their best scowls, too. They looked like the Three Scowling Stooges.

"You got lucky," Billy said. "It won't happen again. I'll be throwing some serious heat this time." He fashioned his thumb and index finger into the shape of the gun and blew on the barrel.

"Ah, the famous smoking six-gun," Connor said with a smile. "I don't know, Billy. That thing was more like a squirt gun last time we faced you."

Billy was turning a lovely shade of red now, which seemed to confuse his two sawed-off associates. They wanted to emulate their leader, but how do you look embarrassed on command?

"Keep making jokes, Psycho Boy," Billy said. "Be a shame if one of my fastballs accidentally hits you when we meet again."

"That almost sounds like a threat," Connor said. "But remember how wild you were last time? You couldn't hit the Atlantic Ocean that day, never mind me."

Billy balled his fists and stomped away, weaving in and out of the other kids in the crowded hallway. He turned one last time to shoot a death stare at Connor, and walked right into an open locker door. Kyle and Marcus were trying so hard not to laugh, it looked like their quivering lips would explode.

Connor grinned and shook his head in amazement.

Then he headed off to science class, marveling at how he was able to control his temper around a knucklehead like Billy, who could make the Pope want to take a swing at him.

Maybe there's hope for me, Connor thought. If Billy doesn't get under my skin, nothing in a baseball game will.

Connor was feeling better about life in general these days. Things didn't seem to be quite as tense at home. His dad was still looking for a job, and money was still tight, but the whole family seemed to be handling it better. His mom had been earning more overtime pay at the hospital, and there hadn't been any more talk of losing the house.

There were other signs of hope. A car dealership across town had called his dad in for a second interview, which everyone seemed to think was a big deal. And Brianna had won a modest scholarship that would help pay for her first-choice college.

It felt good not to be walking around with a knot in his stomach all the time—or suspended from baseball.

As he joined the other kids going into science class, Jordy handed him a note. Connor gave him a quizzical look. "From your new *friend*," was all Jordy said before taking his seat.

Connor moved to the back of the classroom, took his seat, and opened the note.

Hey, Connor!
By now you know I decided to accept your deal. Remember, one more blowup and I will run the story— in print and on the Web. Sports are supposed to be fun.

But you and a lot of other kids seem to be taking these games WAY too seriously.

Anyway, good luck in the playoffs. I'll be watching!

Your friend,

Melissa

Some friend, Connor thought, as he folded the note and stuck it in his backpack.

With friends like her on the sidelines waiting for him to fail, and Billy gunning for him from the mound, he felt like he might as well be going into the last game of the World Series.

Bring it on, Connor thought.

Connor watched his dad climb behind the wheel of the family SUV, fasten his seatbelt, and punch in the address of Eddie Murray Field on the Garmin GPS affixed to the windshield.

His dad tapped GO on the screen. A colorful street map appeared. "Drive to highlighted route," a female voice said.

"Hmm, not bad," Bill Sullivan said. He turned to Connor in the passenger seat and flashed the thumbs-up sign.

"Uh, Dad?" Connor said. "You don't know the way? You've only driven to the field about ten thousand times."

"Yes, I know the way, wise guy. But I'm trying out a new voice." The old voice on his GPS, called American English Jill in the instruction booklet, was too pushy and insistent, he said. When he made a wrong turn, Jill said "Recalculating" in a tone that suggested she was annoyed and mystified as to how he ever got his driver's license in the first place. Hence, this trial run with Australian English Carol.

"In five hundred feet, turn left," Carol intoned.

"Isn't that a nice Aussie accent?" his dad said. "She's *much* less judgmental. You can tell already."

Connor shook his head and grinned. "If you say so," he said, drumming his fingers impatiently on the dashboard. "Now, can we please get going? I don't want to be late."

Actually, there was no danger of that happening, since there was a full hour before game time, and the field was only a mile or so away.

But this was Connor's first game in two weeks, ever since his Black Friday blowup and suspension, and he was eager to see his teammates and play ball. It was also the Orioles' first and long-awaited playoff game. This one was do-or-die against the Yankees—winner goes on to play the winner of the Braves–Red Sox game in a best-of-three series for the championship; loser goes home to sulk.

Connor was so pumped, he had changed into his uniform the minute he got home from school. After that he had grabbed his glove and ball and gone out to the bounce-back net and warmed up for forty-five minutes.

Pre-pregame warm-up, he called it. Hitting the bounce-back net was a good way to work off the butterflies, which were now doing strafing runs in his stomach.

"How're you feeling, buddy?" his dad asked—a little gingerly, it seemed to Connor. "You're just gonna go out there and have fun, right?"

"I'm good, Dad," Connor said. "No need to worry."

His dad nodded and patted his arm. "I'm not worried," he said. "You'll do fine."

Sure, Dad, Connor thought. We're both big fat liars.

When they got to the field, Connor was out of his seat belt and reaching for the door handle before the car even stopped.

"You know I'd stay if I could," his dad said. "But the sales manager at Somerville Ford asked me to swing by. I think they'd love to hire me—if their business ever picks up. But that's a big if."

"I know," Connor said. "Good luck. Let me know what happens."

Actually, until he was sure he had his temper under control, Connor was fine with his parents not being at his games. He leaned over and hugged his dad. Then he bolted from the car and sprinted across the parking lot to the field. The grass had never looked greener, he decided, and the red clay of the infield had never looked more inviting.

As Connor stretched in front of the Orioles dugout, players from both teams began to arrive.

"The big dog is back!" Willie said when he spotted Connor. He cupped his hands around his mouth and turned to the opposing dugout. "Hey, Yankees!" he shouted. "Might as well save yourselves a lot of grief and go home now! You got no chance! The great Connor Sullivan is in the house!"

"Yeah, Yankees!" added Marty Loopus. "You got to worry about another slugger besides me now!"

That one had all the Orioles laughing.

"Way to put pressure on me," Connor said. But secretly he was pleased that his teammates thought so highly of him, even though it made him more nervous.

Just then, Jordy came up and threw an arm around his shoulders. "You're cool today, right?" he said in a low voice. "We're all behind you, you know that."

Connor nodded. Jordy's the greatest, he thought. Always has my back.

"I won't let you guys down again," he said. "Promise."

Seemingly buoyed by Connor's presence, the Orioles jumped all over the Yankees right away. Willie led off the first inning with a single to right, and Carlos Molina doubled him home. Jordy singled Carlos home, and now Connor stepped into the batter's box.

He could feel his heart pounding as he dug in with his right cleat, then the left, getting the balanced feeling in his lower body that told him he was ready.

"Level swing, Connor!" Coach Hammond shouted. More coach-speak for: *Son, I know you're totally jacked up for this one, but don't try to kill the ball.*

But Connor killed it anyway.

Maybe it was weeks of anxiety and frustration coming out, transferred from his brain to his legs and hips and arms and shoulders. Whatever the reason, he took a short, powerful swing at the first pitch, a fastball over the plate. The ball jumped off his bat and screamed over the center-field fence for a two-run homer, making it 4–0 Orioles.

The Orioles dugout erupted, and Connor went into his home run trot. As he rounded third and neared home, he looked up and saw Melissa snapping photos from behind the chain-link fence. Suddenly, she lowered her camera, smiled, and waved.

Connor was so surprised that he started to wave back. Then he caught himself. What would Coach Hammond think of a player waving while he circled the bases after a homer? He could almost hear Coach snorting and spitting out the words "bush league."

The Orioles added two more runs in the third inning

when the Yankees relief pitcher couldn't find the plate and walked four batters in a row before hitting the fifth batter.

"Just throw strikes, Mikey!" came a voice from the stands, probably the kid's dad.

Connor smiled. *Just throw strikes*. That one always cracked him up. As if the kid wasn't trying to throw strikes already. As if he'd hear that and a little lightbulb would go off in his head, just like in the cartoons, and he'd think, Hey-y-y! Strikes! Why didn't I think of that?

The only dumber advice people shouted to struggling young pitchers was, "Just you and the catcher, babe. Pitch and catch!"

Sure, Connor thought. Just you and the catcher—and a batter waving a bat menacingly, and an umpire behind the plate, and seven players behind you, and fifty people in the stands watching your every move.

The Yankees came back with three runs in the fourth inning as Robbie Hammond had control problems of his own, walking two before Mike Messing, their big slugger, belted a homer over the right-field fence.

In the fifth inning, the Yankees threatened again. Their leadoff batter reached on a single to left. Robbie ran the count to 3 and 2 on the next batter, and then reared back and threw him a fastball inside for strike three.

Just then, the runner on first broke for second.

Joey Zinno came out of his crouch behind the plate and fired a perfect throw down to second. Connor moved smoothly in front of the bag, ready to gather the throw for a sweeping tag of the sliding base runner.

Except . . . he dropped the ball.

It bounced harmlessly at the runner's feet.

For a few seconds it was as if everyone—including the Orioles, Coach Hammond, and all the parents in the stands—was holding his or her breath, waiting to see what Connor would do.

And what he did next amazed everyone, including himself.

Scowling, he ripped the glove off his left hand and held it high in the air. But instead of slamming it to the ground, he . . . whacked himself over the head with it.

Then he took a deep breath. And smiled.

"Shake it off, C!" Jordy yelled, and suddenly everyone on the Orioles was chattering at once, telling him: "Hey, nice try, no big deal, we'll get the next guy."

And they did.

Robbie struck out the next batter on a nasty curveball that had the kid bailing out before the ball was halfway to the plate. And the next batter lifted a high fly ball to center that Yancy Arroyo caught for the third out.

As they hustled off the field, one Oriole after another touched gloves with Connor and said, "Good job" or "Way to go." In the dugout, Coach Hammond said to him, "What you did out there, that was a little weird."

Connor winced a little. He knew Coach didn't like any display of emotion on the field.

Then Coach broke out in a smile. "But it worked. Hope you didn't lose any brain cells."

Connor grinned and staggered around like a drunk, making everyone in the dugout crack up.

The Orioles held on for a 6–3 win. As they lined up to

slap hands with the Yankees after the game, Melissa ran up to Connor with her video camera running.

"Nice to see you smiling after a game," she said.

"Nice to *be* smiling," he said. Then he remembered: "So, you going to hold up your end of our bargain?"

"Guess I have to," Melissa said. Connor thought she looked a little disappointed. "But I did get that little glove-on-head maneuver on tape. Can I use that, at least?"

Connor laughed. "Let's see how the rest of the games go. Maybe you'll have a whole reel of Connor Sullivan bloopers to post."

"Hmm," Melissa said. "You know, that's not a bad idea. I'll have to find the right music to go with it. . . . See ya next time, hotshot."

As he watched Melissa run off, her red ponytail bouncing, Connor felt as if he'd passed some kind of test. He wasn't sure if he was more relieved or more tired from burning all the nervous energy he'd stored all day.

All he knew was this: two more wins and the Orioles were champions.

And he, their walking Mount Vesuvius, hadn't erupted— at least, not yet.

"Dude, you smacked yourself! With your own glove!"

"Yeah, that was awesome!"

"It was almost as crazy as Dog Boy gnawing on his shirt!"

It was two days after their win over the Yankees, and the Orioles were loosening up before practice on a field behind York Middle School. Moments earlier, Coach Hammond had gathered them on the bench to announce they'd be playing a best-of-three series for the championship against the Red Sox, who had beaten the Braves, 6–2, behind a two-hitter by Billy Burrell.

The mention of the Red Sox elicited a spirited round of booing. More boos greeted Billy's name, especially when Coach called him "probably the best pitcher in the league—no offense to Robbie, of course."

Naturally, everyone had then glanced at Robbie, who leaped to his feet, held up two fingers on each hand and started chanting, "We're number two! We're number two!" to much laughter.

Now, as they played catch on the sidelines, the hot topic

of discussion was Connor's post-error antics against the Yankees, which everyone agreed belonged on *America's Funniest Home Videos.*

And it might just get there, Connor thought, thanks to Melissa Morrow.

"When you dropped that throw, I thought you'd lose it again for sure," Willie said.

"So did I," Connor said, shaking his head at the memory. "I was *so* mad at myself."

"So how'd you keep from exploding?" Jordy asked.

"I'm not exactly sure," Connor said. "It was like a little voice in my head said 'Stop! Think what you could lose!'"

"You hear little voices inside your head?" Marty said. He pretended to edge away from Connor. "Now you're *really* starting to scare me."

"I know it sounds wack," Connor said. "But it worked. I felt better right away."

"Oh, sure," Willie said, rolling his eyes. "I can definitely see how hitting yourself with a hard piece of leather would make you feel better."

"All right, gentlemen!" Coach shouted. "Big game Friday. Let's do some hitting."

For the next hour, the Orioles took batting practice, with Coach Hammond on the mound throwing fastballs and breaking balls and even a few changeups to keep them on their toes.

Coach had been a pretty good high school pitcher, and he fired the ball in there to each batter, trying to give them a taste of what Billy Burrell would be throwing. Some of the Orioles were hesitant about digging in against Coach—you could see how fidgety they were in the batter's box. But Connor was so locked in he hit three balls over the fence and ripped line drive after line drive with his fifteen swings, causing Coach to grin and shout, "He's tearing the cover off the ball!"

They followed batting practice with a half hour of infield and outfield practice, and then Coach called them together near the pitcher's mound.

"Time to work on our trick play," Coach said.

The Orioles looked quizzically at each other and then back at Coach.

Finally, Jordy said: "Uh, Coach . . . we don't *have* a trick play."

"We do now," Coach said. "We'll call it the 'X Play.' It might even win us the championship; you never know."

They could tell Coach was excited. "All right, pay attention," he said. "We'll use this play when we have base runners on first and third and fewer than two outs. The runner on first breaks for second, okay? Halfway down the line, he's going to trip and fall down."

"Coach, we already have that play," Willie said. "It's called 'The Marty Loopus.'"

As laughter erupted, Marty took a deep, theatrical bow and said: "If anyone needs tips, I'm available after practice."

"No," Coach continued with a smile, "the runner's going to *pretend* to trip and fall. Which means he has to do a really good acting job. And as soon as the catcher throws down to second to nail that guy, the runner on third breaks for home and scores. Everybody got it? Okay, let's practice it."

For the next thirty minutes they worked on the play, each Oriole taking a turn as the runner on both first and third. Coach showed them exactly where on the base path they should trip and fall, and how to make sure the catcher's throw went all the way through to second base before breaking for home.

"The Red Sox could have a trick play of their own to counter our play," he warned. "They could have the pitcher take the throw from the catcher and nail our runner on third. So you have to be heads-up."

Finally, Coach pronounced himself satisfied that they had the play down pat, although he said none of them would win an Academy Award for his tripping performance.

"And here I was hoping you'd be calling me 'Hollywood,'" Willie said with a grin.

When practice was over, Coach gathered them on the bench once more. "Well, this is it, guys," he said. "Just two more wins and we're the champions. We've had a terrific season. But it'll be even sweeter when we beat the Red Sox in this series. Play hard Friday, use your heads, and keep your emotions under control. If you do that, I have no doubt you'll be come out on top. Okay, hands in the middle. . . ."

Connor wondered if that business about keeping your emotions under control was meant for him. But by the time the team huddled up, put their hands in the middle, and shouted "ONE, TWO, THREE, ORIOLES!" he decided Coach was simply reminding all of them to stay calm in the upcoming games, no matter what happened.

As they were leaving the field, they passed the Red Sox

players, who were just beginning to straggle in for their own practice. Leading the way was Billy Burrell, flanked, Connor noticed, by his usual surly mini-posse.

"Well, well, if it isn't the Snoreoles," Billy said when he spotted them. Kyle and Marcus snickered on cue.

"You think that up all by yourself?" Jordy said.

"Yeah, that's a good one," Willie added. "Your brain must be tired."

Billy stopped and glared at them. "You won't be laughing when we're holding the championship trophy," he said. His eyes locked on Connor. "And you, Psycho Sully," he snarled. "I'll be ready for you this time, too. Unless you get thrown out of the game again."

Connor moved toward Billy, then caught himself. *No, stay cool. Deep breath.* He could feel himself getting furious, but all he did was grin. Bullies, he knew, hated when you grinned at them. A grin showed you weren't afraid.

"Nice to see you in a good mood again, Billy," Connor said. "This is two times in a row. That's a personal record, isn't it?"

"Yeah, I am in a good mood," Billy said. "Just picturing that trophy. See you soon, losers."

Billy walked away, Kyle and Marcus trailing behind him like obedient Labrador retrievers. No, that's an insult, Connor thought. To Labradors.

As the rest of the Orioles drifted out to the parking lot to get their rides home, Connor, Jordy, and Marty headed for the bike rack behind the school. There they came upon a disturbing sight: both the front and back tires of Connor's bike were slashed.

A jagged piece of broken bottle lay nearby. Connor bent down to examine it.

"Don't touch it!" Marty said. "The police can dust for fingerprints."

"You've been watching too much *CSI: Miami*," Connor said. "Like the cops are going to drop everything to investigate a kid's vandalized bike." He tossed the glass in a trash can and looked down at the two gaping holes in the knobby rubber tires.

"Who could've done this?" Jordy said angrily, looking around.

"I have a pretty good idea," Connor said, staring back at where the Red Sox were practicing.

"You gonna tell Coach?" Marty asked.

"Nah. No proof. But now I'm even more psyched to play the Red Sox. They're taking this whole thing very personally, aren't they?" Connor unlocked his bike and sighed. "In the meantime, guess I'll be walking. Or riding with Australian Carol."

Jordy looked at him and shook his head. "This new attitude of yours, C," he said. "You sure you didn't knock a screw loose when you smacked yourself?"

"Maybe I did." Connor pulled out his bike. "But at least now Marty isn't living by himself in Bizarro World."

"Hey, welcome to my planet, bro!" Marty said.

Then all three boys laughed as they started walking their bikes home together.

"You're going on a date?" Jordy said over the phone, sounding incredulous. "You're twelve years old!"

"It's not a date," Connor said.

"Let me get this straight," Jordy said. "You're a boy. She's a girl. You're meeting her to get something to eat. At a place in town. But that's not a date? What is it, a dentist appointment?"

"Getting something to eat was Melissa's idea," Connor said. "She even said she'd pay for it. But mainly she wants to take photos of me at the field for her *Tattler* story."

"Yeah, right," said Jordy. "Like she can't wait one more day until we play the Red Sox. And get all the shots she needs. Sorry, bro, but this sounds like a date."

"It's not a date," Connor said. "We don't even like each other."

Actually, Connor wasn't sure that was true. It used to be true. But Melissa had kept her end of the bargain by not posting the video. And since then she seemed to be . . . well, rooting for him. Kind of.

"It's just an interview," Connor said, as much to himself as to Jordy.

After he hung up, Connor stole a quick look at himself in the mirror. His Orioles uniform was clean and ironed, and his cap looked good, pulled low over the eyes with the brim curved and tilted at a slight angle, the way Adam Jones wore his.

It occurred to him that he had never before ironed his baseball uniform or studied himself in the mirror after he put it on. He'd never much cared what he looked like in it, either.

Until today, for some reason.

But it's definitely not a date, he thought as he ran out the back door, grabbed his Rawlings bat, and jumped on his bike.

All they were doing, Connor told himself, was having a slice of pizza at Big Al's Italian Villa. But Melissa offering to pay was definitely key. Connor was broke, as usual. And just the day before, when he had asked his parents about paying for two new tires for his bike, that hadn't gone over real well, either.

"Didn't you get the memo about me being out of work? And money being tight?" his dad had snapped.

Bill Sullivan had just returned from another job interview that hadn't gone well, judging from how tired and discouraged he looked. This one was at a Honda dealership forty minutes away, where his dad said he spent a half hour in the showroom being ignored and drinking stale coffee before the sales manager sat him down for the shortest job interview in history.

But when Connor explained how he had come to find his bike tires slashed, his dad's voice had softened and he shook his head.

"I'm calling that kid's parents," he'd said, reaching for the phone.

"Dad, it's a waste of time," Connor had told him. "Billy will just deny he did it. Nobody saw him do it."

A few minutes later, his dad had put Connor's bike in the back of the SUV and taken it to the local bicycle repair shop, where two new knobby tires were purchased and mounted at a cost of $63.75.

Dad always comes through, Connor thought as he pedaled to meet Melissa. Now if only something would come through for him.

Big Al's was crowded with dinner customers by the time he arrived. He spotted Melissa at a table in the rear, scribbling on a napkin, her backpack slung over a chair. She looked up and smiled when he sat down.

"Tell me you like pepperoni," she said.

"Ohh-kay," Connor said. "I like pepperoni."

"Good," Melissa said, "because I ordered two slices of pepperoni for us. And two Sprites. Maybe I should have waited for you. My little brother says I'm always trying to take charge. He's probably right."

"If you like pepperoni, I like pepperoni," Connor said, which brought another smile from Melissa.

He really hadn't meant to sound so . . . *sappy*. It just slipped out. Jordy would have killed him for that one! He would have said, "C, you're making me gag."

Melissa looked different today, Connor decided.

Different in a really good way. She was wearing a cool Girl Power T-shirt and what looked like new jeans. And there was something happening with her hair, although Connor couldn't figure out exactly what.

While they were waiting for their food, Melissa said, "I want to show you something." She reached into her backpack and pulled out a video camera. After pressing a few buttons, she looked at the display and nodded. "Here," she said, handing it to Connor. "Take a look."

And there it was in all its full-color digital glory: Connor Sullivan wigging out like a middle-school madman in the Yankees game. Sailing that horrible throw to first base, tossing the glove in a rage, snarling at Jordy, whipping the bat against the dugout wall, and then fleeing in tears.

Connor watched the whole thing in silence. Now he was the one who was gagging.

"Well," he said finally, handing the camera back, "that ruined my appetite." Now he was ticked off. Was this whole thing a setup? "What's the deal? I thought you were going to erase that."

For the first time ever, Connor saw Melissa get flustered. "Wait, I didn't mean to . . . I *am* going to erase it, I promise. But first I wanted you to see it. I thought you might want to know what one of your meltdowns looks like."

"Why would I?" Connor said. "I look like a real brat. It's so embarrassing."

"But it's over now," Melissa said. "I swear I'm not going to use it."

Connor couldn't look at her. He felt like getting up and leaving.

"I like the new and improved Connor way better," Melissa said quietly.

That got his attention. She was smiling at him, but her eyes looked sad. "I'm sorry," she said. "That was really stupid of me. I'm going to erase it right now. In fact, here." She gave him the camera and pointed to the delete button. "You can do the honors."

It felt good to trash that file, but Connor was still wary. "How do I know it isn't already uploaded to your computer?"

"Look, Connor," Melissa said, putting both of her palms up on the table. "If I wanted to, I could have spread that video all over the Internet by now. But I didn't. It was a great piece, but I didn't want you to get hurt."

She looked so sincere, Connor had to believe her. "But then why show it to me at all?"

"Like I said, I thought it would help if you saw what you looked like. It would stop you from ever doing it again."

Connor had to admit that, after seeing that footage, he deserved the nickname Psycho Sully.

"Can we start over?" Melissa asked. "I still want to do the story on you. It looks like you guys really might win the championship. And you're the reason why."

Connor blushed. This girl really knew how to make him feel like he was on a roller coaster.

"Yeah, okay," he said, trying hard not to sound like a spoiled brat. "You *are* paying for the pizza, after all."

She laughed, and the tension broke.

After they had finished their pizza, Connor got his bike and the two of them walked over to Eddie Murray Field.

They had about an hour before it would get too dark to take pictures.

Melissa wanted some shots of Connor in his batting stance, so they set up in the batter's box at home plate. Connor held the bat high and waved it in tiny circles. He tried to look menacing, as if he were about to crush the next pitch into another area code. But that was hard to do when you had a pretty girl pointing a camera at you instead of a pitcher like Billy Burrell glaring at you from the mound, ready to throw a blazing fastball under your chin.

"Tell me something," Melissa said, as she snapped away. "Why did you get so angry in those games? I asked your teammates—even took all this video of Marty Loopus, just to get him to talk. And they all said you never had a bad temper until recently."

Connor groaned. "Do we have to go into that again?" He put down his bat. "You never give up, do you?"

"I guess we're both obsessed," she said. "Me with journalism, you with baseball. But I don't get as upset when I make mistakes."

"It was more than that," said Connor. And before he could stop himself, he told Melissa everything—how baseball was his favorite thing in the world, how things at home were tense, how he didn't like everything being out of control . . .

Blah, blah, blah, Connor thought after a while. I'm probably boring her to tears.

But Melissa had been listening intently.

"My mom was out of work last year," she said. "It was

hard. She's a single mom. I had to go to school and then come home and watch my little brother and sister while she was looking for work. Maybe that's why I'm so bossy."

Connor grinned.

"It took her six months to find another job," Melissa continued. "We were all so worried." She shuddered at the memory. "I'm sorry you're going through it. I hope your dad finds something soon. Everyone will feel better after that."

It was getting late. Melissa took a few more shots of him running the bases, and then they said good-bye, with her promising she'd see him at the big game tomorrow.

Riding home, Connor found himself smiling as he played back the last ninety minutes in his mind. It had gotten off to a rocky start, but after that it had been pretty easy to talk to Melissa. In some ways, it was like talking to Jordy or Willie or any of the guys. In other ways it was totally different, which he couldn't quite figure out.

Maybe it had something to do with the way she looked at him.

All in all, he concluded, it had been a fun afternoon.

But whatever it was, it wasn't a date.

Uh-uh, he thought. No way.

Thick, dark clouds hovered as far as the eye could see, and the air smelled moist and earthy as the Orioles took the field for Game 1 of their series against the Red Sox.

"Please don't let it rain," Connor whispered as he trotted out to short and Jordy began throwing warm-up grounders to the infielders. "Not tonight. We want these guys."

The stands were packed and buzzing with excitement, as they had been since both teams finished taking infield and outfield practice. Connor wondered if he had ever been more psyched to play a game in his whole life, with both the league championship on the line and a chance for some payback for Mr. Tire-Slasher himself.

A few minutes earlier, Coach Hammond had gathered the Orioles in the dugout and given them his best pep talk—his "Vince Lombardi speech," he called it, after the old Green Bay Packers coach who had won so many NFL titles. His voice rising and the veins in his neck bulging, Coach had quickly warmed to his subject: we're too good to let anything, even Billy Burrell and his blazing fastball, beat us.

"Be hacking up there at the plate," Coach said in conclusion. "Don't be afraid of this guy."

"Easy for him to say," Marty grumbled. "He's not playing."

At this, Connor had shot a warning glance at Willie and mouthed: "No, don't say it."

Left unspoken was this thought: barring something like a swine flu epidemic raging through the Orioles in the next ninety minutes, Marty wouldn't be playing much, either.

Robbie set the Red Sox down one-two-three in the first inning, throwing crisply and mixing in a nice curveball that had the batters off-balance and flailing helplessly.

When the Red Sox took the field in the bottom of the inning, Billy stepped on the mound and made a big show of glaring at the Orioles dugout for several seconds.

"Play ball, son," the umpire said. "Do that nonsense somewhere else."

As Billy began taking his warm-up pitches, the Orioles glanced nervously at each other. Billy was throwing harder than they'd ever seen him throw. Each pitch seemed to rock the Red Sox pudgy catcher, Dylan, back on his heels. It seemed as if Billy had added another ten miles per hour to his fastball since the last time they faced him.

"The boy's a major-league jerk, no denying that," Willie said in the on-deck circle, chomping hard on his bubble gum. "But he sure can throw smoke."

On Billy's final warm-up pitch, the ball sailed over the catcher's head and exploded against the backstop with a loud *WHAP!*

With a smirk, Billy stared at the Orioles dugout again. "Gee, looks like I'm a little wild today," he shouted.

"Probably not a good idea to dig in, guys."

"Twenty-two, that's a warning," the ump said, using Billy's uniform number. "One more word, and you're gone."

Connor knew that Billy's control was excellent—the best in the whole league—and that his last pitch was designed simply to intimidate the Orioles.

Unfortunately, it seemed to be working on at least one of his teammates. Marty, he noticed, had turned pale. Sitting at the end of the bench, Marty was rocking back and forth with his arms squeezed tightly against his chest.

What was that condition when you were so nervous you couldn't catch your breath? Hyperventilation? Marty looked like he could use a paper bag to breathe into about now.

Yet it seemed as if Billy might have been a little too amped-up himself, because Willie drew a lead-off walk on five pitches. He promptly stole second, causing Billy to stomp halfway to the plate and snarl at his catcher: "Think you could throw even *one* base runner out this season?"

Hidden behind his face mask, Dylan dropped his head in embarrassment and pretended to adjust his shin guards.

"Unbelievable!" Coach Hammond said, shaking his head at Billy's antics. "This kid is the poster boy for spoiled brats. And his coach lets him get away with that stuff!"

Connor felt a twinge of shame. Brat? Yeah, he knew a little something about that.

Carlos Molina went down swinging on a 3–2 fastball, and Jordy struck out on three straight fastballs, talking to himself in frustration as he walked back to the dugout.

Two outs, and Connor was up. As he knocked the

weighted doughnut off his bat in the on-deck circle, he imagined for a moment what it would sound like if the PA announcer was introducing him at Camden Yards: "Now bat-ting for the O-ri-oles, num-ber ten, Con-nor Sull-i-van!"

He took his time strolling to the plate and digging in the batter's box, knowing all this was driving Billy crazy. When it looked as if he were finally ready to hit, he held up his right hand and asked the ump for time. Then he stepped out of the box again, pretending to adjust his batting gloves.

Sure enough, Billy was fuming. His face had turned a deep shade of crimson, and he kicked at the pitching rubber in frustration, imploring the ump to speed Connor along.

Connor hated when guys stepped out of the batter's box during at bats. And he hated having to play this little mind game with Billy. But he knew Billy was a powder keg with a seventy-five-mile-per-hour fastball, and that anything he could do to disrupt his rhythm would help the Orioles.

As Connor had hoped, Billy was so angry now he couldn't even think straight. The moment Connor was ready, the pitcher went into his windup and threw harder than ever.

Ball one, outside.

The next pitch was thrown even harder, with the same result. Ball two.

The third pitch skipped in the dirt in front of the plate, blocked expertly by Dylan, who was lighter on his feet than he looked. Ball three.

Connor stepped out again and took a couple of lazy swings, buying time to assess the situation.

No way he wants to walk me, he thought. He'll take something off this pitch, just to get it over the plate.

He looked down at Coach in the third-base coaching box to see if the "take" sign was on—and was relieved to see it wasn't. Coach was probably thinking the same thing he was: Billy was about to throw a meatball.

Even as Billy went into his windup, Connor knew he was right. Billy had slowed everything down to a crawl, making his movements so deliberate and mechanical he might as well have been holding a sign that said: "Pitcher is about to groove one! Swing from the heels!"

The pitch came in fat and belt-high, as Connor knew it would. He turned on it perfectly and drove a shot into the gap in left-center field. By the time the outfielders had chased it down, Willie had scored and Connor was rounding second base and cruising in with a stand-up triple.

Just like that, it was 1–0 Orioles.

Billy, who had been backing up the third baseman on the play, stomped past Connor and growled: "You're so freakin' lucky. That won't happen again—promise."

Don't say anything, Connor told himself. Let him be the new walking Mount Vesuvius. I'm happy to relinquish the title.

Robbie bounced to first for the final out, stranding Connor at third. But in the Orioles dugout, there was new life. Suddenly the best pitcher in the league looked vulnerable—even if he did look old enough to drive the team bus.

The Red Sox pushed a run across in the top of the third inning to tie it when Robbie walked the first two hitters, and the next batter—Connor recognized him as Kyle, one of the Scowling Stooges—singled up the middle.

But the Orioles threatened again in the bottom of the inning when, with two outs, Carlos drew a walk from Billy, and Jordy hit a slow bouncer that the third baseman booted for an error.

The error seemed to unravel Billy—he stood with his hands on his hips, staring at his third baseman, before stalking around the mound muttering to himself. When he turned back to the plate and saw Connor coming up to bat, a strange look came over his face.

Connor took his time getting set again, digging in with his back foot before stepping in with his left foot.

But this time Billy wasn't about to wait.

Before the umpire could say anything, he reared back and threw his hardest pitch of the night. It was a fastball that seemed to whistle on its way to the plate, darting and rising like a startled hummingbird.

It hit Connor square in the ribs.

He yelped and went down in a heap.

At first he couldn't breathe.

Open your eyes, he told himself. But no, he couldn't—not just yet. It hurt too much, an intense sharp pain in his left side that left him gasping for air and made him think he was about to throw up.

He heard people cry out and run toward him, and now they were bending over him, he was certain of that. But still he couldn't open his eyes.

For an instant he wondered if the ball had gone clean through his body, like a bullet. He didn't feel a breeze. Wouldn't you feel air rushing through you if your body had a big hole in it?

Now he heard Coach shouting, "He threw at him on purpose!" Then the other coach was yelling, and the ump was yelling, and Billy was yelling. Connor wished it were quiet, so he could concentrate on making the pain go away.

Seconds later, he felt a hand on his shoulder, and he heard Coach say gently, "Connor, where did it get you?"

He finally opened his eyes. Coach was kneeling in the dirt beside him, and Jordy, Willie, and Robbie were hovering around him in a semicircle, looks of concern on their faces. Connor tried to point to his left side, where the pitch had nailed him, but the movement made him wince.

"Let's take a look," Coach said now, pulling up Connor's jersey. "Yeah, you've got a nice welt there."

Connor lay on the ground for another minute and felt the worst of the pain gradually subsiding, replaced by a dull, insistent ache. When his breathing calmed down, he tried sitting up, and winced again.

"Easy," Coach said. "Think you can stand?"

Connor nodded, and Jordy, Willie, and Robbie lifted him gingerly to his feet. The crowd gave him a nice round of applause.

"Boys, help him to the dugout," Coach said. "Marty, you're in for Conn—"

"Coach, I'm okay," Connor said. "I'm staying in the game."

Coach quickly shook his head. "No way," he said. "Son, you could have a fractured rib!"

"I'm fine," Connor said. "Look." He made a throwing motion with his right arm. The pain nearly brought tears to his eyes, but he was careful to keep his face expressionless in front of Coach. There's no crying in baseball, he told himself. Wasn't that a famous line from an old movie?

"I don't know. . . ." Coach was saying now. But Connor had already picked up his helmet and was jogging down to first base as the crowd applauded again.

Billy had remained on the mound the whole time, and now he stared at Connor with what looked like a cross between a smirk and a scowl. What would you call that? Connor wondered. A smowl? Whatever it was, Connor couldn't wait to wipe it off his face. *A win today should take care of it.*

What followed was a heated conference between Coach, the Red Sox coach, and the umpire. Connor couldn't hear much of what they were saying. But the gist seemed to be that Coach wanted Billy ejected from the game—and suspended for the next game, too—for throwing at Connor.

"I can't read the pitcher's mind!" Connor heard the ump say. "There's no way to tell if it was deliberate!"

After the conference was over, the Red Sox coach went out to talk to Billy, and Coach Hammond walked over to first base to see Connor.

"I *know* that kid threw at you," he said, still fuming. "But the ump won't do anything about it." He took a deep breath and shook his head wearily. "However, just to show us what a good guy he is," Coach continued, rolling his eyes, "their coach is pulling Billy out of the game. Which he would have done at the end of the inning anyway."

Connor understood immediately. League rules mandated that you could only pitch six innings in a week. Billy had pitched almost three innings in this game. And the Red Sox definitely wanted him to pitch again in Game 2, which is why they had no problem pulling him now.

"So we're gonna have to live with this," Coach said. "How you feeling? Sure you're okay to play?"

Connor nodded. "I'm good, Coach," he said. "Guess we'll just have to beat them without Billy."

Coach grinned and gave him a clap on the shoulder, which woke up the dull ache in his ribs and made him groan. But Coach was already walking back to the dugout, and the new Red Sox pitcher was taking his warm-up throws.

The game was about to resume. Score: Orioles 1, Red Sox 1. Two outs, the go-ahead run on first base. It almost felt like they were starting a new game.

The new Red Sox pitcher was a big, blond-haired kid named Blake. He didn't throw nearly as hard as Billy. But he had a great curveball and quickly put it to use, getting Robbie to bounce out to second base to end the Orioles' threat.

Grabbing his glove and jogging out to short, Connor wondered how well he'd be able to catch and throw. A couple of warm-up grounders from Jordy convinced him he wasn't hurting the team by staying in the lineup. His left side ached, but he felt he could still make any play he had to—as long as Jordy didn't expect a perfect throw to first base.

For the next two innings, Blake and Mike Cutko, who came on in relief of Robbie for the Orioles, settled into a scoreless pitchers' duel.

Now it was the bottom of the sixth inning, the Orioles' last chance to score and avoid extra innings. The wind was beginning to pick up, and off in the distance, the rumble of thunder could be heard. The umpire kept looking nervously at the sky, making sure there was no lightning in the area.

The inning did not begin well for the Orioles. Jordy led off with a bouncer to second for an easy out, and Connor hit a long drive that the center fielder hauled in at the base of the fence. But Blake walked Mike on four straight pitches, and Yancy Arroyo singled to right, sending Mike to third as the Orioles parents cheered wildly.

Here it was: two outs, runners on first and third, a big storm bearing down on them. It was rally-cap time. In the dugout, the Orioles quickly turned their caps inside out and began clapping and stomping their feet, beseeching the baseball gods to deliver a run.

Except maybe the baseball gods aren't tuned in to this game, Connor thought.

Because shuffling to the plate now as a pinch hitter was none other than Marty Loopus.

In the dugout, Willie turned to Connor and said, "Know the five scariest words in baseball? It's all up to Marty."

Connor mustered a grin, but his ribs were aching and his stomach was churning. He was pretty sure his wasn't the only stomach that was churning, though. Everyone on the bench was either furiously chewing gum or furiously chewing sunflower seeds to cope with the tension. Willie had even picked up his glove and was furiously chewing on the dangling leather strings.

Suddenly, as Marty dug in the batter's box, Coach called time-out. He walked down from the third base coaching box and motioned for Marty to join him for a conference. With his arm around Marty's shoulders, Coach murmured instructions for a few seconds. Then Marty nodded grimly and headed back to the plate.

Now Coach was flashing signs to the runners on first and third, touching the brim of his cap, tugging at his ear, wiping a hand across his chest, and touching his elbow.

He was signaling for the X Play! Even though there were already two outs.

But it worked—well, there was no other way to say it—perfectly.

Sure enough, on Blake's next pitch, Yancy Arroyo broke for second base. Halfway down the line, he suddenly sprawled in the base path as if he'd been shot.

Marty pretended to square around as if to bunt, then pulled the bat back at the last second. Seeing Yancy floundering, Dylan, the Red Sox catcher, gathered in the pitch, came out of his crouch, and fired a bullet to the shortstop covering second.

Which was when Mike broke for home, sliding across the plate as the throw from the panicked Red Sox shortstop sailed over his head and hit the backstop.

Orioles 2, Red Sox 1.

Game over.

One more win and the Orioles were champions.

As Mike jumped to his feet and threw his hands up in celebration, the Orioles poured out of the dugout, whooping with joy, mobbing Mike and pounding him on the helmet.

"Did I come through or what!" Marty shouted to anyone who would listen. "Didya see me pull that bat back and confuse the pitcher?"

"You're the best bat-puller-backer I've ever seen!" Willie yelled.

On the outskirts of the mob scene at home plate, Connor spotted Melissa recording it all with her video camera, a big smile on her face. "Are you okay?" she mouthed, pointing to her ribs. But before he could answer, Mike was jumping on his back and screaming, "The X Play comes through!"

Moments later, after the players on both teams had lined up to slap hands amid the first drops of rain, Connor was left with this thought: *It sure would be nice to celebrate this one with the guys, maybe go somewhere and grab an ice cream or a soda.*

But right now he was in the passenger seat of Coach's pickup truck, the windshield wipers slapping rhythmically as they headed for the emergency room.

His ribs were throbbing. His head was pounding. His mouth was bone-dry, and his face was caked with dirt.

Some celebration.

St. Vincent's Hospital was huge, an

imposing complex perched high on a hill overlooking the south side of town.

Years earlier, when Connor and Jordy were driving home from a travel tournament with Connor's dad, they had passed the hospital, and Connor had said casually, "That's where my mom works."

Gazing at the massive buildings, Jordy's eyes had lit up.

"Your mom works in a prison?" he'd said. "That is so cool!"

Connor and his dad had dissolved in a fit of laughter over that one. But looking at the place now as Coach drove through the main gate, Connor had to admit that it did sort of look like the big house, as his dad always called it.

Moments later, he made another observation: when a twelve-year-old kid walks into the ER where his mom works, holding his ribs and looking like he was just run over by a tractor, it will get her attention—and fast.

As soon as she spotted Connor and Coach, his mom's eyes widened. She jumped up from behind the admissions desk and came rushing toward them, a look of alarm on her face.

Coach quickly held up both hands in the universal don't-panic, everything's-all-right gesture.

"He got plunked in the ribs by a pitch," Coach explained. "Don't think anything's broken. Just making sure."

Connor saw his mom's features relax. She bent down and gently put her hands on his shoulders and looked into his eyes.

"You okay, hon?" she said. "Show me where it hurts."

He pointed to where the ache in his ribs was steadily growing worse now. She pulled up his jersey and looked at his side for a moment.

"You're going to have some bruise there," she said. "If it's just a bruise."

The emergency room was busy this evening, as it always was at the start of a weekend, according to his mom.

There was a man holding a blood-stained towel over one eye and a teenage boy holding his wrist close to his chest, as if it might be broken. There was a worried-looking couple taking turns holding and rocking a crying toddler in one corner of the room. There was a little girl with a big bandage on the back of her hand; she had been bitten by a dog, her mother said. And moments later, two young guys in softball uniforms came in supporting a third guy in uniform, who was limping with an ice pack wrapped around his swollen ankle.

But the good thing, said his mom, was that the "loonies" weren't out yet. Connor wasn't exactly sure who the "loonies" were. But Coach said his mom was probably referring to people who always seemed to end up in the ER late at night after drinking or taking drugs and doing something crazy to hurt themselves.

Connor and Coach settled into a couple of hard plastic chairs and spent the next forty-five minutes watching a program called *Top Chef Masters* on the overhead TV.

"A cooking show!" Coach grumbled. "And we can't change the channel. So now they'll have folks here who are hurt *and* bored!"

Finally Connor's mom came over and said: "Okay, let's go see the doctor."

"I'll wait here," Coach said, looking up at the TV. He rolled his eyes. "They're about to baste a chicken. The tension is unbearable. I can't miss a minute of it."

Connor and his mom laughed. Then they went through the double doors and into a cubicle set off with curtains. Connor got up on the examining table, and a nurse took his blood pressure. Moments later, a friendly-looking man in a white coat entered. He introduced himself as Dr. Bill Rose, and he listened to Connor's heart and lungs with his stethoscope before examining his left side.

It made Connor wince when the doctor pressed in certain places. But all the while, Dr. Rose kept up a steady conversation, asking Connor how his team was doing, what position he played, and who his favorite big-league Oriole was, among other things. It helped take Connor's mind off the occasional jabs of pain.

"Okay," the doctor said finally. "Let's get some X-rays."

How long did the whole thing take? Forty-five minutes? Three hours? To Connor, it seemed to take forever. Then he and his mom returned to the cubicle. A few minutes later, Dr. Rose entered, holding the film up against the overhead light.

"Well," he said, "there's the proverbial good news and bad news. The good news is: you didn't break anything."

Connor looked at his mom and saw her give a big sigh of relief. He tried returning her smile, but he was shivering now and exhausted. His ribs were aching worse than ever from all the poking and prodding he'd undergone.

"But," the doctor continued, "the bad news is this: no more baseball. At least not for a while. You've got a pretty good contusion there. We can't risk you getting hit in the same spot. It could do a lot of tissue damage."

Connor was stunned. He looked at Dr. Rose to see if this could be some kind of joke. But the doctor wasn't smiling or winking the way adults usually did when they were joking with kids.

Now Connor's mind was racing. *No more baseball? With the Orioles one game away from the championship? After all I've been through this season?*

"NO!" he shouted.

He jumped down from the examining table. Before he could stop himself, he reared back and kicked the metal wastebasket as hard as he could. It smashed against the table with a loud *WHAM!*

"CONNOR!" his mom shouted.

The sudden movement made his side hurt worse than ever. But that didn't matter now. It was all so unfair! *No more baseball? Why don't they just tell me to stop breathing, too?!*

Angrily, he grabbed his jersey and ran out into the hallway. Already the tears were stinging his eyes. Billy and the Scowling Stooges hoisting the championship trophy?

No way, he thought. I'm playing the next game if it kills me.

Connor didn't wake up until nearly ten o'clock the next morning, after a night spent trying to get comfortable and trying to shut off his brain so he could sleep. Throwing off the covers, he felt a stab of pain in his side, a reminder of everything that had happened since that weasel Billy had drilled him in the ribs.

What a nightmare, he thought.

Immediately after he'd punted the wastebasket at St. Vincent's, his mother had chased him down in the hall and gotten in his face to tell him how disgraceful he'd acted. Then on the ride home, Coach had lectured him on how life isn't always fair, but that you can't get upset and lose your cool every time something doesn't go your way, because it never helps the situation.

"Sometimes," Coach said, "you just gotta suck it up and deal with it."

The truth was, Connor felt worse than anyone about this latest meltdown. He had agonized over it right up until the time he finally fell asleep. Why couldn't he keep his temper in check? Hadn't he been doing so well lately—at least on the baseball field?

Well, maybe. But one thing was clear: he still needed to work on controlling it *all the time.*

As he shuffled downstairs in his pajamas, he heard a strange sound coming from the first floor. It almost sounded like someone was . . . whistling. In fact, it sounded like his dad. He hadn't heard his dad whistle in quite a while—not since losing his job, anyway.

He found both his parents in the kitchen, his dad washing dishes at the sink while his mom made a grocery list at the table.

"Glad somebody around here's in a good mood," Connor said, flopping down in a chair and wincing again.

"Your dad thinks he may have a job," his mom said, looking up and smiling.

Connor eyes widened. His jaw dropped. He looked at his dad, who was nodding and holding up his hand for a high-five.

"Got a call from Hewitt Chevrolet," his dad said. "Big dealership in Ellicott City. Nothing's guaranteed, but it looks good. I have another interview with them Monday."

"That's great, Dad," Connor said. He rose slowly, slapped him five, then gingerly gave him a hug. "That's really great."

As soon as the words were out of his mouth, he knew they hadn't come out with nearly enough enthusiasm.

He was happy for his dad, he really was. But seeing his glove on the counter now—he'd left it there when he came home from the hospital—reminded him that he wouldn't be playing baseball anytime soon. He could feel his spirits sinking fast.

As if reading his mind, his mom said, "I'm glad you're up. Let's talk."

Here it comes, Connor thought, steeling himself. Another lecture about my stupid temper and how I'd better get a grip on it if I ever want to do anything in this life. Well, go ahead. I deserve it. Especially after that ridiculous performance in the ER last night.

"To begin with, Dr. Rose said he felt terrible telling you you couldn't play ball," his mom said now.

Great, Connor thought. Bet he didn't feel nearly as terrible as I did.

"Anyway, he came to see me before I left work last night," his mom continued. "And he had an idea. He said if you could wear some kind of protective padding over those bruised ribs, you'd probably be okay to play the next game."

Connor was still not fully awake, so it took a moment to process what his mom was saying.

When it finally registered, he let out a loud whoop. Then he hugged his mom and did a little dance—no crazy moves; it hurt too much. "YESSS!" he shouted.

Protective padding! Why hadn't he thought of that? Or some kind of hard plastic like big-league batters wore after they were hit on the elbow or the wrist or the shin. He remembered hearing an announcer on the MLB Network say that these days hitters wore more body armor than U.S. combat troops overseas. Why couldn't it work for a twelve-year-old who'd just been drilled in the ribs by a hard-throwing wacko?

But what could he wear that would protect his ribs and still allow him to bat and throw?

Then it struck him: rib pads—what football players wore! They'd work perfectly. He'd wear them inside his uniform jersey. He might end up looking a little like the Michelin Man, but Connor could live with that as long as he could still play ball.

Maybe Jordy's older brother Jack, who played Pop Warner football, had some extra rib pads lying around somewhere. If not, Connor was sure he could get them cheap at Second Time Around, the big used-sporting goods store in town.

He was reaching for the phone to call Jordy when his mom cleared her throat.

"One more thing, young man," she said.

Uh-oh. She wore her Serious Mom face now and was speaking in her No Nonsense tone of voice. Connor knew that whatever was coming, he wouldn't be breaking out any dance moves to celebrate.

"You are to sit down today—right now, in fact—and write a letter of apology to Dr. Rose," she said. "You'll tell him how sorry you are that you acted like a spoiled brat. I'll give it to him tonight at work."

Connor breathed a sigh of relief. He'd expected to hear something far worse—maybe even that he was grounded for flipping out and being so rude to the doc. A letter of apology would be a piece of cake. He'd make it sing, too. Wasn't that what his English teacher, Mr. Korn, was always urging the class to do with their papers? Make 'em sing?

"Oh, and one *more* thing," his dad said. Connor held his breath again. "A girl named Melissa called while you were in the ER last night. Melissa Morrow."

Melissa! But why would she—?

"She wanted to know if you were okay," his dad continued. "You owe her a phone call."

His mom and dad stole a glance at each other. Both were grinning now.

"She's just a girl in my school," Connor said quickly. "So forget whatever you're thinking."

But it left him wondering. Why exactly *had* Melissa called? To make sure he'd be able to play in the next game? Otherwise, it was bye-bye, Connor Sullivan profile.

Or was there something more to it? She had been fun to talk to the other day. Could she actually be concerned about him?

Sure, he'd call her back. No problem! He'd call everyone in the phone book if they wanted him to, now that he could play ball again in the biggest game of the season.

Two more days. Game 2, Orioles vs. Red Sox at Eddie Murray Field. A chance to settle things with Billy. He couldn't wait to see the look on the big guy's face when he showed up ready to play.

Bet the smirk'll be gone, Connor thought. How sweet will that be?

This is how you could tell it was a big game: the mayor threw out the first pitch. And they played a scratchy version of "The Star-Spangled Banner" over the sound system, which kept buzzing and squawking and cutting out altogether.

"Why didn't they do this for the first game?" Willie whispered as the Orioles stood at attention along the first-base line, hands over their hearts.

"They tried to," Coach murmured. "But the mayor showed up late. And they couldn't get the sound system to work."

"Yeah, you see how well it's working now," Jordy whispered, setting off a low ripple of laughter.

Connor was glad to see how loose the Orioles were for this one. Gazing over at the Red Sox along the third-base line, he saw that they had their game faces on. Looking most serious of all was Billy, who kept staring in disbelief at Connor and dipping into a pack of sunflower seeds, apparently trying to set the world's record for most seeds spat during the national anthem.

On the other hand, Connor wasn't totally loose himself, since he was still trying to get used to the rib pads under his jersey. He had borrowed them from Jordy's brother, and taken batting and infield practice with them, but they still felt weird, like he should be playing linebacker instead of shortstop. And he knew the extra padding made him look like a kid who needed to cut down on junk food.

"Okay, everyone over here," Coach said in the dugout as the Red Sox took the field to start the game. "Looks like they're pitching Billy the last three innings this time. Which means we want to jump on their first pitcher, this Blake kid, right away. Men," he continued, pausing for dramatic effect and looking each Oriole in the eye, "let's have some fun and win a championship."

The fun part started early. The Orioles hitters got to Blake right away, and the Red Sox fielders helped matters by suddenly playing like the Bad News Bears—back when the Bears were really, really bad.

Willie led off with a double to right, and Carlos singled him home. Jordy followed with a drive that nicked off the left fielder's glove for an error. To make matters worse, the kid picked up the ball and threw it over the head of the cutoff man. It was finally run down by Blake, who proceeded to throw wildly over the catcher's head, allowing both Carlos and Jordy to score.

Suddenly it was 3–0 Orioles. With no outs.

"Time!" the Red Sox coach yelled, walking slowly to the mound and shaking his head in disgust. He motioned for the entire infield to join him, and ripped into them in a furious voice, wagging a finger in their faces until the umpire finally broke it up.

The Orioles couldn't hear most of what the coach was saying. But at one point they could hear Billy, who was playing third base, snap, "Hey, don't blame me!"

"That's our Billy," Jordy said with a grin. "Team guy all the way."

Now Connor was up, his first at bat ever wearing rib pads. Naturally this did not go unnoticed by Billy, who looked at Connor's billowing jersey and yelled, "Hey, check out this porker!"

Not the most original line, Connor thought as he dug in, his face flaming. But I bet Kyle and Marcus are cracking up.

Blake was rattled—he started out pitching Connor cautiously. He threw two fastballs outside, hoping to get the Orioles shortstop to chase. Then, on his third pitch, he threw the curveball Connor had been waiting for.

The problem for Blake was this: the curveball didn't curve. At least not enough to be effective.

Connor waited until it was belt-high and lashed at it with a quick, short stroke. Later, even though the swing sent a jolt of pain through him, he would wonder if he had ever hit a ball harder in his life. Even before it cleared the fence in dead center field, he went into his home run trot as the Orioles dugout exploded.

As he rounded third base, Connor knew he shouldn't do what he was about to do. Coach would have a fit if he ever found out. But Connor couldn't help himself.

"Oink, oink," he said softly as he trotted past Billy and headed for home.

Seconds later it was 4–0 Orioles, and he was high-fiving and fist-bumping his cheering teammates on the bench. And now he was extra glad he was wearing rib pads, knowing he'd be facing a steaming-mad Billy Burrell on the mound in the fourth inning. I should probably wear shoulder pads and a face mask, too, when he's pitching, Connor thought.

"C, what did you say to Billy out there?" Willie asked. "He was giving you that crazy evil eye again."

Connor shrugged. "I just let him know that even us farm animals can play this game a little."

The Orioles burst out laughing—Connor was relieved to see that even Coach was chuckling.

The Red Sox got two runs back in the second inning on a double by Dylan, their catcher, and a homer by Blake. They added two more in the third when Robbie surrendered a walk and another homer, this one to Billy, who set another world's record, this time for slowest home run trot in history.

"Look at that jerk!" Robbie hissed to Connor as Billy crossed home plate. "Stared at me the whole time he circled the bases!"

"Don't let him get to you," Connor said. "We'll get more runs. Still a lot of game to go."

When the inning was over and they hustled off the field, Coach called another quick meeting. "Anyone ever heard of Yogi Berra?" he asked.

"Sure," Marty said. "Hall of Fame catcher for the New York Yankees. My dad loves all his goofy sayings. Like: 'No one goes there anymore, it's too crowded.'"

Coach nodded. "That's the guy," he said. "Well, his most famous saying is, 'It ain't over till it's over.' And we were playing like this game was over—just 'cause we were up four runs. Well, it ain't over, gentlemen. Let's go out there and play hard."

It was still tied at 4–4 when Billy came on in relief of Blake in the fourth inning for the Red Sox. Billy pitched like his mission was to break eighty miles per hour on the radar gun. He struck out Carlos on three straight fastballs. Each pitch was a blur. Connor half expected to hear cartoon sound effects—*WHAM! WHAM! WHAM!*—as the ball pounded into Dylan's catcher's mitt.

Jordy struck out on three pitches, too, even though he swung early at every pitch—ridiculously early, almost before the ball left Billy's hands.

"Ohhh-kay, the boy is throwing mad heat," Willie said nervously. "Maybe we need the X Play again."

Connor was up. He tapped the rib pads under his jersey, assuring himself they were still there, and stepped into the batter's box. He took a couple of quick practice swings and stared out at Billy.

The boy was smirking. What a surprise.

Billy went into his windup, rocked back, and fired maybe the fastest pitch Connor had ever seen in his life. He could hear the ball rushing toward him—the comics would've labeled this one *WHOOSH!* He started his swing, but it was too late. Way too late.

Strike one!

The next pitch was another fastball—apparently Billy had put his curveball away for the evening—that dipped at the last minute as it split the middle of the plate. Connor swung again. Not even close.

Strike two!

Connor stepped out of the batter's box and took a deep breath. He choked up on the bat, stepped back in, and looked out at Billy. He could see Billy's chest heaving and the sweat glistening on his forehead as he peered in at Dylan for the sign. The kid was so pumped, it looked like he might explode.

Connor gave himself a quick pep talk: *You've hit this guy before. The harder it comes in, the harder it goes out.*

Now Billy reared back and fired another missile. It came in letter-high, the pitch that coaches always told you not to swing at—except they're standing in the third base coaching box and you're the one waving a bat, and you have less than a second to make up your mind.

Connor swung. All he hit was air.

Strike three!

Suddenly he felt it again: the old familiar rage. In the next instant he raised the bat over his head, like a lumberjack raising his ax, ready to bring it crashing down on the plate.

Then he heard it.

"NO!"

Connor looked up.

It was Melissa.

She was standing next to the dugout, her cameras around her neck, eyes wide, one hand clasped over her mouth, an expression on her face he'd never seen before.

She looked scared.

Connor stood there frozen, the bat hovering in the air, eyes locked on Melissa.

She stood perfectly still, shaking her head from side to side, silently mouthing the word, "DON'T!"

And he didn't.

Instead, he lowered the bat and gently tossed it in the direction of the dugout. Then he took off his batting glove, folded it in his back pocket, and slowly walked out to his position as the rest of the Orioles took the field for the bottom of the inning.

"Dude, you had us worried there," Willie said, trotting over and handing Connor his glove. "Looked for sure like you were going to wig out and pulverize the plate."

"Me?" Connor said with a grin. Then he closed his eyes, held out his outstretched palms, and intoned, "Ommmmm."

"Right, you're a swami again," Willie said. "Okay, swami, look into the future. We gonna win this game?"

"Definitely," Connor said. "Don't the good guys always win?"

Well, they do in the movies, he thought. But did it

happen in real life with a kid like Billy throwing lights-out heat?

After taking a practice grounder from Jordy, he looked over at Melissa, who was still standing by the dugout, snapping photos. He waited until she lowered the camera and looked his way, and then he waved. He hoped it looked like a wave of thanks.

But how do you make a wave of thanks look any different from your everyday wave? Connor wasn't sure. Melissa seemed to get it, though. She nodded and waved back.

Mike Cutko came on in relief for the Orioles and immediately ran into trouble. He walked the first two Red Sox batters. Then, desperate to get the ball over the plate, he committed the cardinal sin of pitching: he tightened up and started aiming the ball.

Seeing a nice, fat, slow pitch headed his way, the next batter's eyes widened with delight, and he promptly hit a drive to left field. Marty, in the outfield now that Mike was pitching, misjudged the ball, let it go over his head, and two runners crossed the plate.

Connor felt his heart sink. It was Red Sox 6, Orioles 4.

Coach was chewing even more furiously on his gum now, his jaws working up and down like twin pistons. When he called time and went out to the mound to settle Mike down, Willie and Connor huddled behind second base and exchanged uneasy glances.

"Uh, swami?" Willie said. "The good guys are in trouble."

"A temporary setback," Connor said. "We're still in this."

But he had to admit: right now the movie wasn't turning out exactly how he thought it would.

Whatever Coach said to Mike seemed to work, however. He went back to throwing instead of aiming and blew away the next two batters. And the sixth batter hit a weak grounder to first that Jordy gobbled up easily for the final out.

In the top of the fifth inning, Billy took the mound and threw his warm-up pitches harder than ever. He threw so hard that Dylan whimpered each time the ball cracked into his mitt, taking the mitt off to shake his stinging left hand.

In the Orioles dugout, Coach watched Billy grunting on every pitch, and shook his head. "No way he can keep throwing that hard," Coach said. "He's going to burn his arm out."

In fact, once they stepped in against him, the Orioles could see that Billy's velocity was decreasing already.

Mike worked the count to 3 and 2 and went down swinging on a pretty good fastball. But Yancy roped a hard single to right. Marty followed with his usual bouncer back to the pitcher for the second out. Then Joey Zinno hit a rocket that caused the Orioles to leap off the bench and cheer—until it tracked right to the Red Sox center fielder for the third out.

They were still behind by two runs. But in the Orioles dugout, there was a flicker of hope now. At least Billy seemed mortal again. The smirk was still there, but the overpowering fastball wasn't. And Coach was smiling his I-told-you-so smile.

"Hold them here," he said as they hustled out to the field. "We'll get to him next inning."

But Mike Cutko struggled with his control again,

walking the first batter on four pitches and hitting the second batter on the ankle.

As the kid hobbled to first, and the Red Sox manager called time to make sure his player was all right, Connor and Willie trotted to the mound for a conference.

Mike was normally a reliable pitcher with great control. But now he seemed agitated, pacing around and kicking at the dirt with his head down.

"I'm killing us," he moaned.

"You're *not* killing us," Willie said, draping an arm around his shoulder. "But if you don't put the ball over the plate, *I'm* going to kill *you*."

Mike looked up quickly to see if Willie was kidding. But there wasn't a hint of a smile on the second baseman's face.

"Well, at least you didn't put any pressure on him," Connor said as they trotted back to their positions.

"Sometimes," Willie said, "the direct approach works best."

Whatever the reason, Mike seemed to come out of his funk again. He reared back and struck out the next two batters. Then he got Billy on a two-hopper to first that Jordy gloved easily before stepping on the bag. Billy didn't even bother to run the ball out. Instead, he stopped a few feet down the base line, tore off his batting helmet in disgust, and skipped it into the Red Sox dugout.

As he walked off the mound, Mike pointed at Willie and flashed a big grin.

"You really have a way of motivating people," Connor said as they hustled off the field.

"Learned it from my momma," Willie said with a laugh.

"That's how she motivates me sometimes."

Now it was the top of the sixth, the Orioles' last chance to score.

"Let's go, now," Coach said. "We got the top of the batting order up. And Billy's on fumes."

But for one of the few times the Orioles could recall, Coach was wrong. Connor could see that Billy was still throwing hard. Maybe not crazy hard like before, but hard enough.

Yet somehow Willie managed to coax a leadoff walk, and Carlos followed with a perfect drag bunt down the first-base line for a base hit.

Two on, no outs, Jordy Marsh coming to the plate. Now it was the Red Sox dugout that stirred uneasily. Standing on the top step, their coach rocked back and forth nervously, both hands tucked in the pockets of his jacket.

Jordy worked the count to 3 and 2 and smacked a vicious line drive to left—the hardest shot since Connor's first-inning homer. But it was right at the left fielder, who barely had to take a step to make the catch.

On the mound, Billy raised both hands in triumph, as if to say *Look at me, see how well I'm pitching? I got the batter to do that.* Even his teammates rolled their eyes at that one.

Now Connor was up. As he took his last practice swings in the on-deck circle, Coach spoke to him quietly.

"You know Billy's going to gear it up for you. Whatever he's got left in the gas tank, he'll use it now. Be patient. Short, compact swing."

As Connor walked to the plate, Billy stood off to one

side of the mound, rubbing up the baseball and trying to stare him down.

Amazing, Connor thought as he dug in. *The kid's arm is about to fall off, and he still has major attitude.*

Billy went into his windup, kicking his left leg high, and fired a fastball down the middle. It wasn't his best heat, but it was plenty fast enough, especially for a kid with a supposedly sore arm. But Connor was taking all the way. Strike one.

Billy's next pitch was nearly identical, a fastball with even more zip on it, but still Connor kept the bat on his shoulder. Strike two.

Now Connor stepped out and took a couple of practice swings, trying to anticipate what Billy would throw next. This was the mental chess game between batter and pitcher that he loved so much.

Then it hit him: *He wants to embarrass me. Wants to strike me out on three pitches. He'll come back with the exact same fastball. In the exact same spot.*

Which is exactly what happened.

This time Connor was on it, everything moving as it should, hips, arms, and shoulders opening in a perfect symphony of a swing. The ball soared into the gap in left-center and rolled all the way to the fence as Willie and Carlos crossed the plate.

By the time the left fielder tracked it down, Connor was flying around second base. The kid's throw sailed over the cutoff man, and Connor kept digging around third even as Billy scrambled to retrieve the ball in front of the Red Sox dugout.

Billy snapped a throw to Dylan, who was blocking the plate with one leg. Connor went into his slide, felt a sharp jolt of pain from his rib as he hit the ground. Dylan hooked the ball into his mitt and tried for a sweep tag as Connor reached under him and grazed the plate with his left hand.

"Safe!" cried the umpire.

For a moment, Connor lay there on his back, listening to the cheers from the stands, waiting for the awful ache in his ribs to die down. Then he saw a hand reaching down to help him up.

"Nice hit," Billy said quietly as he pulled Connor to his feet.

Connor was too stunned to speak.

Then Billy snarled at his catcher: "You can't make a better tag than that?" and stalked back to the mound.

Connor lurched to the dugout, holding his side. Had Billy really said something nice to him? He wondered if the pain was making him hear things.

But maybe there was another side to Billy. Connor thought back to his own behavior these past few weeks. Maybe there was trouble in Billy's life that was causing him to lash out at people.

The rest of the inning went by in a blur. To the Orioles, it looked like Billy's arm was screaming at him now. He could barely reach the plate with his next few pitches. Somehow he got Robbie, the next batter, to fly out to center field, and Yancy grounded out to second base for the third out.

But the damage was done.

Orioles 7, Red Sox 6.

Three more outs and they'd be champions.

Jogging slowly out to short, Connor found himself whispering: "Just hang on, Orioles." He had never wanted to win a game more in his life.

Winning the championship would make up for a lot of things. It would make up for all the tension at home after his dad's layoff. It would make up for all the crappy weeks when he was having meltdowns that nearly got him kicked off the team.

It would even make up for his not being able to attend the Brooks Robinson Camp, which he wanted to do more than anything else in the world.

Connor knew the Orioles hadn't nailed the game down yet. A one-run lead was nothing. The Red Sox hadn't made it to the championship game because they stunk. They weren't going to just lie down and die.

But Mike had found his groove now. He looked focused and relaxed during his warm-up pitches, the ball popping into Joey's mitt with authority. Briefly, Connor wondered if Willie's "death threat" had actually worked. A new coaching technique! Whatever. Mike looked ready to go out there.

And he was.

He struck out the first Red Sox batter on a nasty 2–2 curveball that broke sharply at the last minute and had the kid swinging at a ball in the dirt. The second batter hit a weak grounder to second that Willie gobbled up easily, throwing him out by ten steps.

The Red Sox were down to their last out.

Now the Orioles were a picture of concentration, each player on his toes and locked in on the game, the noise from the stands growing louder and louder. For the Red Sox, it was all up to Dylan. Their stocky catcher had some pop in his bat. Coach motioned for the outfielders to move back.

"Don't leave the ball up, Mike," Connor said to himself. "Not to this guy."

Mike pitched Dylan carefully. Ball one was low and away. Ball two was inside. Now he had to put one over the plate. And Dylan knew it.

The big catcher stepped out and took a practice swing. He dug his right foot in the batter's box, stepped back in with his left foot, and held the bat high, waving it in tiny circles.

Mike went into his windup. This time he threw a fastball, belt-high, and Dylan uncoiled with a vicious swing. Connor heard the crack of bat meeting ball and held his breath. But instead of a long drive to the outfield, Dylan hit a towering pop-up behind third base.

Connor and Carlos drifted back, both of them calling for

it, tapping their gloves with their fists as the ball fell from the deep blue sky.

Connor's side was throbbing. For an instant, he wondered if he'd be able to raise his glove hand to make the catch. He started to shout to Carlos, "You take it!"

But now they heard the sound of running footsteps behind them and another voice—a shrill, insistent voice—screaming over and over: "I got it! I got it!"

At the last second, a skinny arm with a glove attached to it appeared over their heads.

Marty Loopus leaped high in the air and caught the ball. Crashing into Connor and Carlos, he stumbled for a moment, squeezed his glove closed, and held it high over his head.

Then he yelled as loud as he could, "WE DID IT!"

Game over. The Orioles were champions.

They came from every direction, cheering and screaming and jumping on Marty. Jordy landed on him first, and Willie followed. Soon they were all tumbling to the ground and laughing. Connor fell on top of the pile, not caring anymore about the pain in his ribs. Looking up, he saw Melissa standing a few feet away, smiling and snapping photos of the whole raucous celebration.

When they finally untangled themselves and walked off the field to more applause from the stands, Connor heard a familiar voice calling his name. Looking up, he saw his dad, giving him the thumbs-up sign. Mom and Brianna were there too, grinning and waving. He waved back, pumped his fist, and howled.

Then he wondered, What's Dad doing here? Does that mean he . . . ?

But Connor would think about that later. Right now he wanted to enjoy this perfect moment.

Maybe the most perfect moment of his life.

Big Al's Italian Villa was quiet when Connor arrived. A couple of college kids were eating meatball subs at the counter, and an old man sat on a nearby stool sipping a milk shake. But most of the staff seemed to be wiping down tables and filling salt and pepper shakers and napkin holders in preparation for the dinner-hour rush.

Melissa waved to him from a booth up front.

"Thanks for coming," she said when he sat.

"You sounded pretty mysterious over the phone," Connor said.

"Didn't mean to be," she said. "But I have something I think you'll want to see."

"Oh, no," Connor groaned. "Not more video of Mount Saint Connor erupting."

"No, nothing like that," Melissa said. "I see you're still paranoid, though."

"Before we get started," Connor said, "tell me you still like pepperoni."

"If you like it, I like it," she said, smiling.

"Good," he said. "Because I ordered two slices of

pepperoni and two Sprites when I walked in."

Connor had been happy when Melissa asked him to meet her at Big Al's. As he'd told Jordy, who again insisted this was some kind of date, he didn't consider Melissa to be a girlfriend.

Just a friend. Who, um, happened to be a girl.

This time Connor even had money to pay for their pizza, thanks to his dad, who had slipped a ten-dollar bill in his hand as he walked out the door.

For the first time in months, he could be a big spender today. He might even have enough left over to spring for ice cream for dessert. Well, *one* ice cream, anyway.

But that was okay with Connor. In fact, everything was okay now that his dad had started his new job with Hewitt Chevrolet and a sense of calm had returned to the house.

His mother was smiling again—"I feel like going over there and kissing Bob Hewitt on his big, bald head!" she'd said at dinner the other night. This was at a Chinese restaurant—the first time they'd eaten out in months—and Connor couldn't remember the last time his family had seemed so happy.

Brianna had spent the whole meal chattering about all the plans she was making for college. There had even been talk of Connor attending the Brooks Robinson Camp in a few weeks. Dad had said he wasn't sure if they could swing it financially just yet, but he'd look into whether Connor's slot was still available.

"A big star like you, they'd be crazy not to hold a spot open," his mom had teased.

At that moment, Connor couldn't decide which he liked better: the General Tso's chicken or his mom's sunny mood.

Now, when their order arrived, Connor and Melissa ate and talked about the Orioles' wonderful season, about their big win over the Red Sox a few days earlier, and about Billy Burrell and what a jerk he'd been.

"Then he's nice to you after your hit!" Melissa said, shaking her head.

"Yeah," Connor said. "I want to talk to him. Maybe something's bothering him."

"Or maybe he just felt guilty about hitting you with that pitch," Melissa said, taking a bite of her pizza.

"I bet it's more than that," Connor said. "Hey, I was a jerk at times, too. I'm just lucky I found a way to control my temper—before it was too late."

"Speaking of which . . ." Melissa said.

She wiped her hands with a napkin and reached down for her backpack. Unzipping one of the pockets, she pulled something out and threw it on the table. It was an early copy of the *York Tattler*.

Before he could look, she scooped it up and held it behind her back.

"Okay, the big Connor Sullivan story's in here," she said. "So let's play a little game. It's called 'guess the headline.'"

"That's easy," Connor said. "Head Case Shortstop an Embarrassment to the Game."

Melissa shook her head. "Still don't trust me, eh?"

"Or maybe," Connor continued, "Why Does League Put Up with This Brat?"

"Okay," she said, rolling her eyes. "This is hopeless."

She tossed the newspaper to him and folded her arms.

Connor stared at the front page headline: "Youth Baseball Star Plays Game the Right Way." Underneath was a smaller headline that said: "Orioles infielder makes team proud," with the byline, "by Melissa Morrow." And under that were three photos: Connor ranging to his right for a ground ball against the Red Sox, Connor smashing a home run off Blake in the second game, and the jubilant Orioles celebrating after the final out.

He read the first few paragraphs and looked up. Melissa was grinning.

"Thanks," he said in a soft voice. "It looks like a great story. Better than I deserve."

For a moment he was silent.

Then he smiled and pointed at the photo of himself hitting the homer.

"But you *had* to run a picture of me in those rib pads!" he said. "*Had* to make me look like the fattest kid ever to play baseball!"

"Hmmm," Melissa said, pretending to examine the photo. "I don't think you're wearing rib pads there."

"What?!" Connor said. "No way!"

"Yeah, I think you're just getting a little chunky," she said. "Maybe you need more exercise."

Now both of them were laughing and teasing each other, and Connor was hoping he had enough money for ice cream, too, not wanting the afternoon to end.

Not that this was a date or anything.

Because it definitely wasn't.

Uh-uh. No way.

If you enjoyed this book, look for

Super-sized Slugger

a novel by
CAL RIPKEN, JR.
with Kevin Cowherd

Cody braced himself for the usual reaction. It was the first day of practice for the Orioles of the Dulaney Babe Ruth League, and Coach Ray Hammond was going down the line, asking each kid to say his name and the position he wanted to play.

"Cody Parker. Third base," he said when it was his turn.

From somewhere behind him, he heard snickers.

Here we go, he thought.

"Third base, eh?" Coach Hammond said. He studied Cody for a moment.

Cody knew what was coming next. Coach would try to break it to him gently. *Why not try the outfield, son? You're a little, um, big for third base. In fact, I'm thinking right field would be perfect for you.*

Everyone knew the unspoken rule: right field was for fat guys. And slow guys. And guys with thick glasses and big ears and bad haircuts. If you smacked of dorkiness at all, or if you looked the least bit unathletic, they stuck you in right field, baseball's equivalent of the slow class. Then they got down on their knees and prayed to the baseball gods that no one would ever hit a ball your way in a real game.

That's why Cody hated right field. Hated it almost as much as he hated his new life here in Dullsville, Maryland, also known as Baltimore, where the major league team stunk and people talked funny, saying "WARSHington" instead of "Washington" and "POH-leece" instead of "police."

No thanks, he thought. Give me Wisconsin, any day.

Immediately he felt a stab of homesickness as he thought about his old house on leafy Otter Trail. He pictured his corner bedroom on the second floor with the wall-to-wall Milwaukee Brewers posters, especially the giant one of his hero, Prince Fielder, following through on a mighty swing to hit another majestic home run. He saw the big tree house in his backyard, and the basketball hoop over the garage, and the trails in the nearby woods, where he used to—

"Cody?" Coach was saying now.

Cody shook his head and refocused.

"Okay," Coach said. "Let's see how you do at third."

Hallelujah! For an instant, Cody thought of giving Coach a big hug. But Coach didn't seem like the hugging type. He was a big man with a short, no-nonsense crew cut and an old-fashioned walrus mustache. He looked more like the hearty-handshake type. Except his hearty handshake could probably crush walnuts.

Minutes later, the Orioles broke into groups for infield practice. Trotting out to third base, Cody was surprised to see he was the only one trying out for the position.

Then he heard the sound of heavy footsteps behind him and felt a sharp elbow in the ribs.

"Out of the way, fat boy," a voice growled.

Wonderful, Cody thought. The welcoming committee is here. Looking up, he saw a tall, broad-shouldered boy he recognized as Dante Rizzo.

"Instead of 'fat,' could we agree on *burly*?" Cody said, smiling.

That's it, turn on the charm, he thought. Kill 'em with laughter.

"Shut up and stay out of my way," Dante said, spitting into his glove and scowling.

So much for trying the charm, Cody thought. But the truth was, he *didn't* consider himself fat—not in your classic Doritos-scarfing, Big Mac—inhaling, look-at-the-butt-on-this-kid sort of way.

His mother said he was big-boned. It was his dad who called him burly. To Cody, burly was preferable to big-boned, which sounded like he had some kind of freak skeletal disorder. Cody thought he was built along the lines of the great Prince Fielder, if you could picture the Brewers' first baseman as a thirteen-year-old with a thick mop of red hair and freckles.

Big, sure. Even chunky. But nothing that made you wrinkle your nose and go, "Ewww."

On the other hand, Dante obviously didn't share this assessment of Cody's body type, which came as no great surprise. Cody thought back to the first time he had met Dante—although *met* might not be the right word—on his first day at his new school, York Middle.

Cody had been eating lunch, sitting in the back of the cafeteria with a few other kids, mostly nerds and misfits who seemed just as lonely as he was. Suddenly, something warm and moist smacked him in the back of the neck. It turned out to be a soggy pizza crust.

Whipping around, Cody had seen a tall boy with long dark hair smirking at him and nudging his buddies.

"Congratulations," the kid sitting next to Cody had said. "You've just been introduced to Dante the Terrible."

"Yeah," another kid had added. "He's in eighth grade and he's fifteen—draw your own conclusions. His hobby is pounding people. And if you mess with him, he's got two older brothers who'll mess with *you*."

"Vincent and Nick. We call them the Rottweiler Twins," a third kid had chimed in. "On account of they're so warm and cuddly."

Remembering the pizza incident now, Cody shot a nervous glance at Dante. Just my luck he plays baseball too, Cody thought. Why can't he play lacrosse like every other kid in Maryland?

And what are the odds we'd both end up on the Orioles? And be trying out for the same position?

About the same as the odds of my being confused with Prince Fielder, he decided.

Coach picked up his black fungo bat to begin hitting ground balls to the third basemen, and Dante elbowed Cody aside.

"Back of the line, rookie," he said. "Veterans go first."

"My boyish good looks don't count?" Cody said.

At this, the rest of the infielders covered their mouths with their gloves to hide their smiles. Cody wasn't sure whether they were laughing *with* him or *at* him.

Dante glared and shook his fist. "I thought I told you to shut up," he growled.

Great, Cody thought. I'm the new kid. I'm a little out of shape. And now the local thug wants to use me like a piñata.

Maybe this was Dante's second year with the Orioles, and maybe he had played third base last year, but he was an awkward infielder, anyone could see that. He was a good two inches taller than Cody, yet he crouched way too low and took short, clumsy strides to each grounder, bobbling the first two. As a big guy himself, Cody sometimes felt he had all the mobility of the Washington Monument.

But he knew the key was to take advantage of your height and strength to cross over and move laterally.

One weekend last year, in fact, he had watched YouTube videos of every big third baseman in the major leagues, just to see how they set up and moved to a ground ball. "How come you don't study this hard for science class?" his dad had asked. And the short answer was simple: it wasn't baseball. Nothing in the world got Cody excited like baseball.

The other thing Cody noticed was that Dante's throws to first base tended to sail. This was because he never set his feet properly. Only a couple of great leaping grabs by the first baseman—a rangy kid with terrific hands—saved the throws from going over the fence.

After botching yet another grounder, Dante slammed his glove to the ground and cursed loudly.

"Language!" Coach yelled, shooting Dante a look. "We had this problem last year." Dante kicked angrily at the dirt and muttered under his breath. A couple of players shook their heads.

"All right, Cody," Coach said. "Your turn."

"Don't let the pressure get to you, lard-butt," Dante whispered.

"Remember: I'm *burly*," Cody whispered back, earning another death stare. "I thought we went over this."

Now Cody sensed that all eyes were on him, the way they always were whenever he had to prove himself on a new team. It was always: *Let's see what the big guy's got— probably nothing.*

He dropped easily into his crouch, weight balanced evenly on the balls of his feet, body tilted slightly forward to get a jump on the ball. He punched the pocket of his glove and straightened the brim of his cap, at the same time marveling at how relaxed he felt.

This was what he loved about baseball: how comfortable he always felt when he stepped across the white lines. Everywhere else he felt like a dork—a *giant* dork—most of the time. But never on a baseball diamond.

"You're always smiling when you play ball," his mom had said once. And why not? Cody thought. Baseball's easy. It's the other stuff in life that gets complicated.

He gobbled up the first four grounders hit to him and made strong throws to first each time, earning a nod from Coach. But Cody could tell he was about to be tested. They always think it's a fluke when the big guy looks good, he thought.

Sure enough, the next ball was a scorching two-hopper to his right. He dove and snared the ball backhanded at the last second, kicking up a cloud of dirt. Quickly, he scrambled to his feet and fired a bullet to first.

"Not bad!" Coach yelled. "Almost made that look easy!"

The last ball was another shot, this time to Cody's left, in the hole between shortstop and third. He took three quick steps, lunged for the ball, and spun 180 degrees before whipping a strong throw to first.

The kid at first nodded and pointed his glove at Cody, as if to say: *You da man!* "Hey!" Coach said, grinning now. "That's a big-league play right there!"

"You got lucky, fat boy," Dante muttered from a few feet away as Coach moved on to hit grounders to the shortstop. "No way you're that good."

Cody shrugged and said nothing. That was the other thing he loved about baseball: the chance to prove people wrong, make them shut up. He'd been playing the game since he was, what, six years old? How many times had kids made fun of his weight, then stared slack-jawed when he back-handed a hard shot at third or legged out a double with a headfirst slide? The name-calling tended to stop pretty quickly after that.

Besides, he thought, the big leagues were full of ter-rific players who didn't exactly look like they lived on salad and granola bars. David "Big Papi" Ortiz with the Boston Red Sox. C. C. Sabathia with the New York Yankees. Pablo Sandoval with the San Francisco Giants. Adam Dunn with the Chicago White Sox. There was a time when fans might have blamed steroids. Now players just seemed to be big-ger and stronger, and a lot of that came from their work in the weight room.

After hitting balls to everyone, Coach announced that it was time for batting practice. He grabbed his glove and a bucketful of balls and headed for the pitcher's mound.

"Everyone gets ten swings," he said. "Make 'em count, boys."

Hearing this, Cody pumped his fist and thought, *Yessss!* He loved playing third base, but hitting was his favorite part of the game. He could have had a bad day at school, his mom and dad could be on him about his messy room, his mind could be buzzing with a hundred different thoughts, but as soon as he stepped into the batter's box, he felt calm and focused. It was an amazing transformation — maybe not as dramatic as what Spider-Man or Thor went through when they went from supergeek to superhero, but close.

The Orioles broke into hitting groups. Right away, everyone saw that Coach was throwing some serious heat. He was pitching from a full windup, and even though his control was good, the ball was whistling as it smacked into the backstop.

Cody noticed that few of his teammates seemed eager to dig in.

"Hey, ease up, Coach!" Dante yelled when it was his turn. "Let the big dog hunt!"

"You guys want me to throw underhand?" Coach said in a mocking voice. "Maybe we can get the Braves to throw underhand for the season opener too."

Cody shagged balls in the outfield until Coach finally waved him in to hit with the last group.

Right before he was up, Cody unzipped his equipment bag and pulled out his bat. Then he carefully wiped it down with a towel. Just looking at the bat made him smile. It was a beauty, all right: silver with red flecks, a thirty-one-inch, twenty-one-ounce birthday present from his mom and dad. If you held it at just the right angle, with the sun glinting off it, it looked like a flaming sword as you walked to the plate.

He gripped the bat, brought the barrel to his lips, and glanced around to see if anyone was looking. Then he whispered, "Time to go to work, buddy."

He wasn't sure when he first took to talking to his bat—it had been a couple of years now. He guessed he did it for good luck—not that the bat always listened to him. And he probably did it to calm himself down at the plate too, and help him focus. But this little ritual wasn't something he wanted to share with his new teammates just yet.

He could imagine the reaction: *So you talk to your bat, huh, Parker? And what does Mr. Bat say back? Does he tell you to lay off the high fastball? Or: don't swing at anything in the dirt?*

That's all I need, Cody thought. People thinking I'm fat *and* crazy.

As he dug in against Coach and took a couple of warm-up swings, he stole a glance at the short left-field fence. It looked so inviting for a right-handed hitter, like there was a big neon sign out there flashing the message: HIT IT HERE! Forget the fence, he told himself. Start trying to jack home runs to impress Coach and you'll mess up your swing, big-time.

Instead he focused on the mantra his dad had preached for years: "Short, level swing. Just hit the ball somewhere — and hit it hard."

As it had so many other times, the advice paid off. Cody roped the first three pitches for what would have been clean singles and followed that by driving two balls into the gap in left-center field. On the sixth pitch, as often happened when he was swinging well, he smashed a long, soaring drive that cleared the fence in left field by ten feet.

Now Cody heard excited murmurs from the Orioles ringed around the backstop behind him.

"Whoa!" one kid said. "Tagged!"

"Big kid has game!" another voice said.

You like that? Cody said to himself. Watch this!

But this time he swung too hard at the next pitch, swung from his heels, missed it completely, and almost fell down, the way Prince did sometimes. Then the big man would climb back in the batter's box and flash a sheepish grin that seemed to say *Kids, don't try that at home.*

"Felt the breeze back here, dude," a third kid said as the others chuckled.

Relax, Cody told himself. Don't lunge at it. Wait for it. And this time he turned on the pitch perfectly, smacking another shot that easily cleared the fence in left. Now the murmurs grew even louder.

After he whipped around to see where the ball landed, Coach let out a whoop.

"Boy has some thunder in his bat, doesn't he?"

Big kid comes through, Cody thought, more relieved than anything.

When practice was over, Cody was tired and hungry. But he was pleased with how he'd done the first day with his new team. As he walked off the field, the lanky kid who had made the great plays at first base tapped him on the shoulder.

"You're the new kid, right?" he said. "I'm Jordy Marsh. You looked pretty good out there."

"Thanks," Cody said. "You looked pretty good yourself. Way to get up for those high throws."

Jordy smiled and leaped in the air, pretending to throw down a ferocious dunk. "Yeah, I'm a regular Kobe Bryant when I have to be," he said.

Now they were joined by another boy. Cody recognized him as the brown-haired kid who had taken most of the balls at shortstop, effortlessly vacuuming up one hard shot after another.

"Connor Sullivan," the kid said, giving Cody a fist bump. "Boy, you were killin' it in practice today."

Cody looked down and scratched idly at the dirt with his spikes, searching for something to say.

"Coach was probably taking it easy on me," he said finally.

"No way," Connor said. "Coach wouldn't take it easy on his own grandmother. You were dialed in, dude."

Jordy and Connor jogged off, saying they'd see him in school the next day. Seconds later, Dante ran by and jabbed another elbow into Cody's ribs.

"Do yourself a favor, fat boy!" he shouted over his shoulder. "Find another position!"

Terrific, Cody thought. Eleven other kids on this team, and I have to play the same position as the budding middle school hit man. Who is definitely not happy now that I showed him up.

Cody changed out of his spikes, gathered up his bat and glove, and began the long walk to the parking lot, where his mom would be waiting in her car.

The late April sun was setting. The tall pine trees that ringed Eddie Murray Field cast long shadows everywhere. He shivered slightly in the damp air.

He had a feeling he'd be seeing a lot of Dante Rizzo from now on.

Which might not necessarily be a good thing.